RETURN OF THE FIREFLIES

Laura Hollowell

ISBN: 978-0-578-74180-2

Cover design by: Katie Green K.T.Digital
Library of Congress Control Number: 2018675309
Printed in the United States of America

Light

The night has a thousand eyes
And the day but one;
Yet the light of the bright world dies
With the dying sun.

The mind has a thousand eyes
And the heart but one;
Yet the light of a whole life dies
When love is done.

FRANCIS WILLIAM BOURDILLON

CONTENTS

CHAPTER 1

I t's never really quiet. I mean the kind of quiet that makes you feel uneasy; glancing over your shoulder quiet; pin-drop quiet. You know, like...silent. There's always some noise to tune out whether it's the refrigerator, the ringing in your ears, atoms bouncing off one another...never really *silent*. The air conditioner just shut off and at first the absence of noise is heavy and obvious for only a few seconds until the symphony of cicadas creeps into my awareness. You though, you are a different kind of silence. Your absence screams at me over the AC unit and the insanely noisy insects. Your absence fills up my thoughts, my ears, my space, my life with its booming, blankness; its empty void. You won't turn off and I can't tune you out.

Now there's just one cicada chirping in rhythmic pulses and I focus on it as cars splash by in the distance. By most anyone's standards, it's quiet here; however, most measures of quiet do not include you but mine do and I remember every little sound, every little nuance of your voice, your presence. By most measures it is quiet here...*most* measures.

You must have known this was coming someday. I don't imagine what I have to say will be surprising even after all these years. I just can't hold it in any longer. Patience is a virtue I guess, but not for me. It keeps me satisfied – stagnant, waiting for you to show up in some magical, fairytale return and here I am, still holding out.

I know I should be over you by now and this seems crazy. I guess some people really do find their true love at sixteen. Romantic and sweet? Hardly. It's been more like a curse waiting all these years, but this waiting is killing me. What I want to do is tell you how I really feel. It would go something like this: "I miss you. I still love you and it's looking like I always will." I don't know why I feel this urgency now. Maybe it has something to do with the way time is flying or maybe I'm just finally speaking up for myself. Either way, this is what I want, what I've always wanted - the day when waiting for you ends and my life with you finally begins.

I wonder if you're still the same after all these years. Is your voice still soft and deep? Do you still have that high-pitched laugh when something's really funny? Is your skin still tight and flawless? Is your personality still the same or have life's disappointments tamed you?

I have proven to myself over the years that I can make it on my own. I have a college degree, a career, a car, a cat, and I even go on vacation sometimes, but in spite of all this, as complete as I seem, I am living a half-life haunted by all the ways you are not here.

In a couple of hours I will turn another year older. Ok, let's be honest...thirty-eight. On this birthday, I am giving myself the gift of action. I am going to do what patience has kept me from doing. I'm asking that you remember me...that you consider me again. On the other hand, if my feelings are truly unrequited, then I need you to help me let go before I completely fade away

2

into this false hope.

The last time I saw you, you were turning left at an intersection with my first replacement sitting in your passenger seat. I was only eighteen then. Now, twenty years later, maybe it's finally time for me to make my last stand before I'm too old to get up.

You are my first love and a damned hard one to let go so I've just been holding on since the night I met you on Judd Street in 1989. And the sickest part of my ego - the hopeful, patient part - tells me you never really let go either. Most likely, you will never read this letter so I'll just keep it in case my patience runs completely out and it somehow finds its way to you.

Lucy

****

So this is it, my letter's final draft. I've rewritten it many times but no more. This one is the last. I've come to a crossroads in my life, a reality check, really. I figure this is my final push to the end considering I live out my life-expectancy; a life that has so far been defined by waiting for the man I love to return to me. For twenty years I have waited and yes, there were times when some primal instinct pushed me out in search of his replacement, but I always found one fatal flaw- they were not him. So I have decided that in order to survive the remaining years of my life I must remove these memories from my mind by transferring them to these pages in hopes of discovering an exit, a release, an awakening...although I'd really just settle for a little peace and quiet.

CHAPTER 2

****

Patience –
My Protector
"God's Will will be"
Well, patience has deceived me
The long road ahead lies barren, unexplored
While I've been waiting at this lonely door
Patience will bring you back to me
I've been faithful to these memories
All these years, waiting so long
And I've always been wrong.

If you love something let it go and if it comes back, then it was truly yours. These words meant something to me even as a little girl. They were a promise between me and the fireflies I would catch in my quart jar when they flew from our honeysuckle hedge showing off their talents in a spectacular twilight show. I could slip out the back door unnoticed, escaping my father's rage and my mother's tears, into the calm, quiet, plush carpets of grass, swaying curtains of weeping willows, and star-spangled chandelier sky that created a perfect theatre for my little friends' dance during those sweltering summer North Carolina nights. I thought it was better to set them free after they took a short rest in my jar. It felt like letting go was the right thing to do and I figured they would just die or at least be unhappy in their new confinement if I kept them closed up in the tiny glass world I had prepared with a leaf and a few blades of grass. Anyway, it didn't matter because my same fireflies, after given their freedom, faithfully returned to my backyard theatre each summer for another brilliant performance.

Now that those summer nights are just fading memories, I find myself clinging to the words, "if it comes back." I need them to give meaning to more than just my childhood firefly fantasy. I need them to actually work, to come true, to make sense of my love story. I need them to make sense of my life. I'm sure I followed the directions hidden in the message – fall in love, let him go because you're too young, too inexperienced to know better, and then he'll come back at the perfect time. Simple, right?

Despite the years, I still believe our love story will eventually be defined by those treasured words. I wonder though, was it really as magical as the faithfully returning fireflies of my childhood? Will he be as faithful as they were? At this rate I'll just be waiting and aging until gravity pulls the last grain of sand to the bottom of my hourglass.

It seems so strange that a little girl who understood the importance of letting go would spend most of her life holding on; holding out for some magic hidden behind a cliché. Well, for now, that magic is all I have. It gives me a sense of peace when I think of my age and how I haven't been able to recover since my only love put me out on the corner lot and drove away all those years ago. Now, I walk through life alone while couples sit across from each other at little round tables eating ice cream, hold hands on a walk down the beach, teach their kids proper T-Ball posture when up to bat. No, really, it's ok. I ward off panic by repeating my mantra, "I'll be ready when he comes back."

There is a love story behind this melodramatic soul-sopping so please bear with me: *Two young lovers found each other by a stroke of more than luck, by a twist of more than fate. Whatever force it was that brought them together couldn't compete with human nature; it was that which tore them apart.*

We were destined to be something we have not yet become, and I am still waiting because as long as his heart beats, whether or not it belongs to me anymore, it's looking like my stubborn heart will always belong to him.

CHAPTER 3

****

Two seeds tossed by a gentle breeze
Lightly landing side by side on soft, fertile soil
In a vast expanding landscape
Under the same sun, under the same moon
Sharing the same air, the same wind, the same rain
Learning to grow, to give, to live
Learning to love

My memories of the days before I met him are all clouded behind the fog of Robert Smith's wailing vocals and the smoke from clove cigarettes that lingered heavily in the air. I was riding my sister's social train because I didn't have one of my own. Talking to others was hard when I just really had nothing to say. It was like my mom and dad had only a limited amount of personality to pass on to their offspring and the one who came before me used it all up. This deficit didn't lend itself to popularity. Mary, the one who came before me, had a magnetic personality. She was nineteen and had just recently moved away from home to live in a house on Judd Street with a few friends in our sprawling strip-mall, military town in the Sandhills of North Carolina. It was easy for her to make friends so I relied on her social skills. She was the girl everyone knew and loved; the most popular, fun girl in the crowd. But she had a strong rebellious streak that led to her full submersion into the gothic culture of tattoos, piercings, drug experimentation, and music obsession. This rebellion was born and nurtured through years of trying to be "Daddy's little girl." That never happened because, with our dad, it never could and she wouldn't forgive herself for not being enough to get his fatherly love and affection. She never understood that with our father, it didn't exist. In contrast to Mary's billboard screaming, "LOVE ME!!!!" mine whispered, "leave me the hell alone."

Even with her flaws, I envied Mary's ability to connect with people and marveled at her various levels of conversation. I wanted to be with her and loved her with all the blind admiration of a little sister in spite of all the reasons not to. I wondered how she had so much to say. Something as simple as, "Hey, what's up?" was tricky for me because of the towering brick walls I had built from years of existing below the radar. So I watched; the meticulous onlooker in the corner who spent time observing life, not really participating in it.

I found entertainment there on Judd Street just by hanging back and taking in the sights which always consisted of black clothes, black hair, black eye-makeup, and red or even black lipstick all worn on androgynous Goths. All of this was barely visible through a sort of surreal kaleidoscope of candle lighting and clouds of smoke. What I heard was loud music with intense lyrics that somehow crept into my soul underscored by the low murmurings of the Judd Street housemates and their select after-party visitors. Underneath it all, a melancholy cry for help. These certainly were intriguing nights for the budding recluse I was already becoming at the ripe old age of sixteen.

To my sister's friends, I was just a sweet, quiet girl if they even noticed me at all. I was the smart violin playing introvert who sat pensively and spoke only when spoken to. But I was Mary's little sister so I was loved and accepted on Judd Street. My straight *naturally* black hair hung down past my shoulders. I didn't usually wear makeup or clothes that would have labeled me into any group, just jeans and a t-shirt at best. I certainly did not look like I fit in on Judd Street. There was not one thing about me beyond average. In fact, I was strikingly normal.

Each time I arrived on Judd Street, I would feel the brief popularity of being Mary's sister. "What's up, Lucy?" I'd hear from the dimly lit living room already beginning to fill with "social rejects." At least that's what my parents called them. On the contrary, I found Mary's friends to be more than just "rejects;" they were fearless, cordial, and committed to self-expression.

Andrew, a tall, lanky redhead was the oldest of the housemates at twenty-six, and the self-appointed resident "mother" of Judd Street. He didn't dress like the Goths or cover his face in make-up. It was like Andrew was there to supervise and take care of his housemates. He catered to my shy and innocent nature. Each time I came over he made an all-out effort to hide or throw out all the beer bottles and cigarettes.

"Get the hell out of here with that cancer stick! What's wrong with you?"

Andrew would bark off to offenders all the while spraying them down with air freshener. Then he'd turn to me and say,

"You don't need to be around that stuff, baby."

Pan was tall, quiet, hunched-over, and skinny with pale white skin and jet black hair that hung over his worried blue eyes. He would sit right on the floor, never in a chair, and occupy himself for hours with a fine-tip black marker and a journal filling its pages with his words and sketches. We would make eye-contact. He would signal me with a nod to come sit by him on the floor. Then he would lean over to share his latest strokes of gothic genius with me while Andrew eyed us disapprovingly.

With every visit to Judd Street I found my way to the empty corner chair. I was listening, watching, and never ceasing to be amazed at the flow of interesting people passing in and out of the old, wooden, rambling two-story house with a front porch and an A-line roof. It was an antiquated building that perfectly contrasted with its progressive residents. I always had the delusion when I was at Judd Street that I was somewhere better than I actually was.

****

I could practically feel the earth spinning that chilly autumn night before my life took an unexpected turn. Something just felt different yet I almost chose to ignore it and stay home in spite of the mysterious urgency brewing inside me. It was normal for me to hide out from the world in my tiny, solitary bedroom but on this night I felt an insatiable desire to go with Mary. She had come home for a short visit that included dinner and laundry and was leaving for Judd Street. I ran out of my room yelling, "Mom, I'm going with Mary!" and then went running through the front yard, waving my arms to catch her before she drove off in the silver station wagon our parents let her drive. I didn't wait for permission. This was a night planned for me by the Gods and I was playing right into their demanding hands.

Unexpected and unlikely visitors entered the Judd Street house several hours after Mary and I arrived. Andrew had invited a group of three soldiers from the 82nd Airborne to party on Judd Street after a night of dancing to a loud mix of 80's alternative goth-rock and techno at Club Nevo, our pitiful city's hangout for the growing population of "social misfits."

Club Nevo was a light gray metal garage-type structure masquerading as a real building. Inside was a pulsing, thriving night club complete with black lights, smoke machines, and chain link fencing along the walls. During my first visit, I walked right in behind Mary and Andrew, took a barstool and spent three hours feeling the music vibrate into my bones while practically choking from the onslaught of synthetic smoke. I was mesmerized by the small dance floor packed with Goths glowing under black lights all doing the same sort of lumbering gothic stomp in time to the throbbing music.

These soldiers would have stood out among the usual Nevo crowd since their outfits contained color and their overall look was more frat house than Judd Street. He was the last one of the three soldiers to enter. At first glance, I saw his typical soldier buzz cut and his eyes squinting to see through the foggy concoction of clove, candle, and cigarette smoke. White sweatshirt, blue jeans, big black leather high tops – untied; wide nose, cupid-bow lips, suntanned face – skin splotchy-red with embarrassed self-consciousness. As I glanced around the room, I wondered why everyone wasn't looking at him. No one else even noticed him. How could it be that this level of human perfection existed among the rest of us? How was it that the entire world wasn't in love with him? How could anyone be in his presence and not be overcome with his beauty; his shy, unsure demeanor? Ok, I get it...cupid's arrow was particularly toxic that night.

With his head down, shoulders hunched a little, and nervously scratching at his little bit of blonde hair, he glanced around the room and disappeared from view while his friends mingled.

After those intense seconds, I wondered if he had noticed me sitting Indian style in my lonely corner chair. Had he noticed my jeans and cream-colored shirt with embroidered flowers around the neckline standing out among all the black clothes? I wondered if I stood out to him as someone who didn't belong in that gothic living room on Judd Street. Was he feeling that way himself? I chuckled and thought how funny and strange that I could feel my pulse returning to normal as if I had just run the fifty-yard dash sitting right in that chair. It was a strange sensation, seeing for the first time, the man I would love for the rest of my life.

A quick glance to the floor beside me revealed Pan's distressed expression. A once blank page in his journal now illustrated a sad story. A black heart floating above a raging black sea. Blackbirds flying from the heart's shattered core filling the white sky. A hopeless, lonely hand desperately reaching out from the tempest.

"Um, Pan. Are you ok?"

His ability to slam a journal closed and sulk away was an art form perfected.

For the rest of the night, I did my usual eavesdropping on deep conversations and observing social interactions but I was really waiting for one more glance; one more adrenaline rush. I waited as long as I could until the party became too crowded for my comfort level and forced my escape upstairs to Mary's room.

CHAPTER 4

I soon learned where he had disappeared to during his first hours on Judd Street. He had been hiding out from the growing crowd in Tory's room. Her parents owned the old house and allowed her and a few of her friends to live there. Tory had an infectious laughter that could fill up any space and could often be heard above the music on Judd Street bringing a smile to even the most cynical Goth. She emitted an aura of jovial friendliness even though her appearance told a different tale: thick black eye make-up, many ear and facial piercings, platinum short spiky hair, ripped fishnets, and fingers adorned with silver rings, and black fingernails of course. Tory was Mary's best friend and my co-worker at the Record Exchange. She looked like she would work there; me, not so much. I was the youngest employee at the hole-in-the-wall record shop and was glad to have the opportunity to make a little money for my-self. My mom was just happy for me to get out of my tiny room for a little while and be a part of the real world.

I found that working at The Record Exchange was more fun than actual work. Sure, I would buy and sell music but mostly I would just hang out with my co-workers while we watched and mingled with our faithful, music-loving customers. There was the Volkswagen-bus-driving-surfer-mechanic who came in religiously and with each visit bought five to ten CDs from various artists ranging from Skinny Puppy to Miles Davis. We also served the neurotic Frank Zappa type who meticulously eyed the used vinyl for imperfections only to rant and rave about how some idiot had ruined the vinyl's integrity and decreased its value and collectability; and how insane we were for having bought such below-standard tripe from the individual. James was our favorite heavy-metal music lover; a large man with an impressive mullet which he wore with pride. Another one of my co-workers, Arthur, had taken a Polaroid of James' mullet every time he visited our store. This collection of pictures entitled "James' Mullet" was a living, growing piece of art that hung in our back room. Arthur, like Tory, appeared to be born to work at The Record Exchange with his authentic grunge attire and his "I-just-don't-give-a-fuck" attitude. He was an indie guitar-playing, garageband leader who lived and breathed all things music.

One slow weeknight Tory nudged me behind the counter and said, "I have a secret about you, Lucy," (insert laughter).

"Well, what secret could you possibly have about me?" I replied half-heartedly.

"I know someone who likes you," she said in a taunting voice knowing how easily embarrassed and shy I was.

"Ha! Yeah, right," I laughed and rolled my eyes in disbelief of anyone having a crush on me. I let her continue and quickly fantasized that it would be *him*.

"Well, I'm not kidding," she said with a serious tone. Her lack of infectious laughter caught my attention. For some reason my mind shifted to that first night I saw *him* disappear in the depths of the Judd Street house. She began a description. "Remember when Andrew invited those army guys to Judd Street the other night?"

I shrugged, "I guess."

"Do you remember the really cute, shy one with the red cheeks? He asked about you when we were talking. Anyway, his name is Connor and I'm pretty sure he wants to meet you."

I took a deep breath as my face changed to scarlet and shook my head with embarrassment as tears welled up in my eyes and chill bumps covered my arms. I was pissed off that my body refused to cooperate with my need to be discrete. There it was, his name: Connor. I replied jokingly, "Thanks a lot, Tory, for letting me know. Now I'll be sure to make an ass of myself in front of him."

We both laughed partly because we knew it was mostly true, but also because there was the potential for something new and exciting to begin. Obviously unable to fake indifference, I headed off like a deer in headlights to alphabetize the cassette wall.

CHAPTER 5

Friday night at nine-thirty, Mom was there to pick me up from work. On the way home, she offered Taco Bell to which I gladly agreed. Over a cheese quesadilla and a Diet Pepsi, I asked, "Can I spend the night with Mary?" sort of blurting it out. I knew I had to get to Judd Street somehow to see if Connor would show up. "I mean, I know it's a hike, but could you drive me over there after I grab my stuff?" I shamelessly asked of her.

"I guess. It's kind of late to be going out though."

"Well, I'd like to go if you don't mind taking me. And anyway it's not really 'going out;' it's just Mary's."

"All right, but try not to wake your dad up while you're packing."

"Deal," I said nodding my head. I guess she felt a little sorry for me because I didn't really have any close friends from school. I preferred to stay in my room writing, practicing violin, reading, or listening to music when I was home, and since Mary had moved out, I was more withdrawn than ever. This is probably why she was happy to assist me with some social interaction even if it was at that "house of horrors." Once we were home, I carefully selected one song from my small collection to inspire the right mood for the night. Morrissey's brooding self-depreciation always seemed appropriate for me: "Please, please, please let me get what I want this time."

Careful what you ask for.

I chose to wear my black vest with five buttons down the front, a black cardigan sweater that would reveal just enough, and my black stretchy pants with black Dr. Martens. My long, straight hair and "Hint of Red" lip gloss topped-off my best Judd Street look. While throwing some jeans, a t-shirt, and an old hooded jacket in an overnight bag, Mom stood at my door and asked, "So, who are you dressin' up for? Looks like you're wearing your sister's clothes now."

This annoyed me beyond reason. "Mom, please. I... I think... I guess I'm ready to go now," I said, taking a quick glance around my room and then darting out the front door to the car. Finding out about Connor's potential crush on me had elevated my confidence but I believe I was more empowered by fate. I was planning to do something completely against the grain of my personality; initiate conversation with a gorgeous male whose acquaintance I had not yet made. This definitely had to be fate.

The moon was full and cast a haunting glow around the little house which made it look just as spooky as some of the characters inside. The red pickup Connor had arrived in last week was parked right in the front yard so there was a really good chance he was there. I said in a hurry, "Thanks, Mom. Be careful driving home. I'll get Mary to take me to work tomorrow. Love you." "All right, love you too," and she pulled off. I walked into the Judd Street house that October night feeling different. I was on a mission, excited, and compelled to action but unfortunately, I had no idea what to do.

Judd Street was in progress as partiers crowded the living

room, dining room, and kitchen. I didn't see him among the black clothes, the spiked hair, and the silver chains so I hid out in Mary's room for the night with Evan, one of the Judd Street housemates, discussing Joyce, Yeats, and how the disbandment of The Smiths still physically hurt. We were a great pair tonight in our gothic attire but mostly because he did all the talking while I halfway listened. Where was my nerve if I possessed any? I hoped that I was making Connor wonder where I was. I knew that he must have seen me or at least heard Mary's house-mates greet me when I arrived. Certainly, he must have heard Andrew's sudden outburst of morality as he attempted in vain to clear the living room of "heathens" when I walked in. Was Connor too shy himself to come talk to me? Why didn't I just go find him and claim him? I was in full-game mode playing "mystery of the pursuit" and losing.

Later, when all was quiet, Evan was sleeping soundly on the floor and I had given the game a full-blown shot at working, I grabbed my gray hooded sweater and crept down the stairs. I turned the corner to find five after-party stragglers passed out on the living room furniture. The front door had been left wide open exposing the old house to a chilly autumn draft. I closed it and stood there shivering for a moment. The house was strangely still and silent. Dusk was on its way but darkness lingered. A faint light coming from the kitchen caught my eye as I was looking for any sign of life, feeling depressed that my ama-teurish game had failed. Reflecting on this moment, I clearly see how fate offered me a fork in the road: seek out the dim light or return back up the dark staircase. Twenty years later it is still not clear to me if I made the right choice.

I headed toward the dim light. As if in a dream or a scene from a movie there he was, alone...a gorgeous figure leaning against the sink holding a glass half-filled with water. The light which had drawn me in was coming from the pantry, barely shining through the black sheet that was hanging to replace the missing door. Even still, I could see that his faded green sweatshirt was tight-fitting especially around his upper arms and that his old 501 jeans had been worn to comfortable perfection. I could see that his big high tops were untied. My instinct was to run in the opposite direction but I was not in control. I confidently moved toward him operating on autopilot.

"Hey, I'm Lucy Bells. I'm Mary's sister. She lives here." I looked down and shook my head feeling so idiotic just wishing I had something more profound to say at this most important moment.

Still leaning against the sink, he gulped down his swig of water and choked, coughed, and with his fist beating a little too forcefully on his broad chest, squeaked out, "Yes, I know, I'm Connor...(clears throat)...Hawthorn. Hi."

He extended his hand and received mine for a shake still patting his chest with his other hand. My heart was racing and I knew, I just knew. Our love story was already written in the stars before we met. If I had known right then how it would end, would I have had the strength to walk away? The answer is decidedly, no.

"Are you from here originally?" he asked as his face faded from completely to splotchy red.

"No. I mean mostly from here, I guess but I've moved some," I said.

"So, you're in high school?"

"Yeah, I'm a junior, eleventh grade. I guess you can already tell this town pretty much sucks, huh?"

"Yeah, I guess, but I think it's got potential," he replied, eyes scanning me from head to toe. "Have you been here all night? I didn't see you earlier."

And just then, before I could answer, the front door opened and an impatient voice yelled,

"Connor, move out!" to which he quickly replied, "Hooah!"

Through a somewhat disappointed expression he said,

"My, umm, friends are waiting for me outside so I need to...go. But I hope to see you again soon, okay?"

With his hands jammed in his pockets and one last green-eyed glance over his shoulder, he was gone.

My reply rose from the bottom of my throat and fumbled out too late for him to hear, "O...Okay."

I stood there for too many minutes after he left feeling ridiculous in my Judd Street attire covered by an old worn-out hooded sweater. Now I was useless. Just like that, my mind was overcome with thoughts of him. I imagined us sitting in the Judd Street living room, in the smoky, dim lights, contrasting with the people around us discussing all that we had left to share. But would he even show up on Judd Street again? I was consumed with teen obsession which is, I guess, a common reaction for a sixteen-year-old girl. This obsession, however, would singularly last the rest of my life.

I've read somewhere that the reason we can't see the future is because we wouldn't be able to survive the next hour with the burdensome knowledge of what will come to pass in our lives. Not knowing the future allows those of us who desperately cling to the past to be ignorantly hopeful of days to come. Ignorance truly is bliss. I am a living example of this since the moment I laid eyes on Connor Hawthorn.

CHAPTER 6

Mary came early to pick me up after a slow Friday night at The Record Exchange. We had been hanging out with Arthur blasting Soundgarden's "Louder than Love" in the tiny red and black rectangular space filled to the brim with all things independent and underground. Arthur put down his air guitar, picked me up off my stool, spun me around, and said, "Go ahead, I'll close up." After a full week of replaying over and over that twenty second conversation during my first meeting with Connor all I could think about was the possibility of seeing him walk into the Judd Street house again.

Once we arrived, I passed the time surface cleaning the house with Andrew, and attempting to stifle the butterflies in my stomach. He would have lectured me about military boys so I didn't dare let on to him that I was anxiously waiting to see Connor, if he even showed up. I watched Mary and her housemates as they decorated themselves in what could only be described as Halloween outfits and enjoyed the soundtrack including Depeche Mode, Nine Inch Nails, and Mary's favorite, The Cure. The rolling bass line from "A Forest" filled the house with a somber, perfect gothic pulse. It was almost distracting enough for my nerves to watch Mary tease her black hair into a sort of fireworks design and then spray to hold for a night of praying on her knees in the middle of the dance floor to her idol, Mr. Smith. Her red lipstick was purposefully smeared just a little in his honor. Then she and her friends headed off to Nevo to pay homage to the music that shaped their way of life.

Before the after-party crowd arrived, I was ready with my book, my journal, and a nonchalant posture. It was like I belonged there, but as a social scientist making cultural observations on a different species. Pan had taken a seat on the floor beside me but I could not be bothered with him tonight. My mind was occupied with one thing only...

Finally, our eyes met as he entered the house. He looked straight at me as if he had been waiting for that moment to see if I would be there in the shadowy corner. Without even glancing around, he made his way over to me and sat on the arm of my chair. He spoke directly into my ear so that I could hear him under the music. "That was hell," he said trying not to yell. I supposed he was referring to the hours he had just spent at Nevo dancing among the Goths. My heart was practically pumping out of my chest.

The smell of his cologne and the warmth of his breath close to my face was both sensual and masculine. Trying to keep my composure, I just laughed for no apparent reason. "I was wondering about that actually. You don't really seem like the Nevo type. So, what brings you to Judd Street again?"

He laughed now, dropping and shaking his head as if he was about to do or say something he might regret. "Well, I guess I was kind of hoping you'd be here, and that if you were here my torturous evening wouldn't be a complete waste." I looked up at him and smiled. He raised his eyebrows and shrugged.

I wanted him to myself, away from the noise and the growing

crowd, so I headed out the front door gesturing with my head for him to follow. We sat on the porch steps wrapped in a humid post-rain fog while the scattered moon light illuminated the low-lying clouds around us. I unloaded more words on him that evening than I had ever spoken on Judd Street. It must have been my nerves and acute fear of awkward silence that kept the information flowing. I told him a little about my parents and my reasons for hanging out with Mary on Judd Street. I delved into my favorite foods and music groups. I talked about The Record Exchange and the unbearable days spent at Howard Massey Sr. High. I told him that I was on the track team and that I had come in second place for the two-mile run during my last meet. I let him know that I believed in God and that I had never smoked but had recently tasted beer and thought it was disgusting. He chuckled.

This must have seemed like a confessional instead of a first real conversation. I wonder what he might have said if my insane rambling had allowed him an opportunity to speak. He seemed content to listen which was a skill he had obviously perfected. He never interrupted, always made comfortable eye contact, and nodded at the perfect time. He delivered raised eyebrows, flexed brow, and courtesy chuckle when appropriate. The only time he spoke about himself was when I asked specific questions. Selflessness appeared to be his overwhelming character trait. And after all my involuntary self-indulgence, he held my hand sandwiched between both of his and said, "I am so glad I spent those torturous hours at Nevo." He smiled, winked at me, and kissed me on the cheek before he stood up. He held out his hand to help me stand and stood aside so I could enter the house first. Within a couple of minutes, he and his army buddies were gone. But first, I had just enough time to scramble together a pen and a paper towel from the kitchen. I wrote my phone number and gave it to him on his way out. "Thank you. I'll need this," he said with a cool half-smile and was out the door.

Who knows what waited for them on the base: physical training, cleaning barracks with a toothbrush, dangerous training mission? I had no idea. I missed him more than I could bear; I knew that for sure. I missed the way he smelled of cologne masking hints of machine oil and bleach, the way his body radiated warmth, his emerald eyes and soft tan skin, his quiet, deep voice. I collapsed in my comfy corner and watched as the party burned off like the fog outside. Curled up on my oversized chair in the dark corner, I finally slept and dreamed of Connor.

CHAPTER 7

For three weekends in a row, Connor showed up on Judd Street to see me. We had also been talking on the phone in brief, heart-stopping moments when he would call just to say, "I hope you had a great day. Sweet dreams." And they were sweet; every night dreaming of our first kiss. Then finally...

My memory has captured this particular night as if we were actors in a movie. The scene begins as we escape from the growing Judd Street crowd to Tory's room during a particularly loud and creepy rendering of "Bela Lugosi's Dead." A single box spring and mattress were on the floor with a black comforter neatly pulled up over black sheets and black pillowcases. Throw pillows in purple and red added a touch of color to the room. A musical jewelry box with a tiny ballerina mounted atop was neatly placed on a bookshelf lined with old literature textbooks, journals, and worn paperbacks ranging from Austin to Whitman. A rocking chair in the corner was draped with an old quilt; not really items one would expect to see in a girl's room who donned black fingernails and ripped fishnets. Some elements in Tory's room posed a contradiction in this house just like Connor and me.

We nonchalantly ignored the light switch when we walked

in allowing the closet light, which was already on, to suffice. While sitting beside each other on the mattress we tried to avoid yelling over the music which just resulted in nervous, awkward smiles. It was impossible to ignore the elevated tension between us. Thankfully, one of Tory's two cats that roamed the house came wandering in. She slowly made her way over to us and leaned her body, purring, against Connor's leg. He reached down, gently picked her up, and placed her in his lap. In the dim light, the cat's white fur and Connor's white button-down shirt seemed to glow. I thought how lucky I was to be there with him and how unlikely it was that of all the girls who would have loved to keep him company on Judd Street, he continued to choose me. I looked at the illuminated cat and reached over to rub her sleepy head.

I had touched his hand before but this felt different. When my fingers brushed his, it sparked such a physical reaction that it caused me to be embarrassed. My heartbeat accelerated so much that I was sure my shirt had a pulse of its own the way it was bouncing with the pounding I felt inside my chest. An adrenaline surge caused the hairs on my arms to stand. Our eyes met and just as I was thinking, "does he feel this too?" the back of his fingers stroked my left cheek. My eyes closed. I felt his hot breath and then his soft warm lips pressed against mine. My entire body was wrapped in a blanket of chills. I trembled under the pressure.

"I'm sorry. I should have asked first."

In response to his apology, I reached up with both hands, touching his scarlet cheeks which were hot as fire. I was closing in for another go because I had to feel that one more time, but before I could seal the deal, light flooded the room as if there were a director calling, "CUT!"

"Oh, Hi Lucy. What's up, Connor? Not interrupting anything I hope." (Insert infectious laughter.)

"Tory, no, of course not. We were just...talking...and anyway, have you seen Mary?" I was up and out of the room, brushing past a smiling Tory before our "first kiss scene" could properly end.

I heard him leave soon after that. I closed my eyes deep in a corner of Mary's room and prayed to be enough for him; for this to be more than just another sweet dream.

CHAPTER 8

C onnor had arrived at Fort Bragg six months earlier from Savannah, Georgia after enlisting in the army at the age of eighteen. At first, his army buddies had to force him off the base to "loosen up" since his narrowly focused agenda did not include socializing. He saw Ranger school, Delta Force, or whatever posed the most difficult challenge. Now he was coming to Judd Street willingly.

Getting to know Connor was easy. He was funny, self-conscious, and well-mannered. He was also confident, proud, and a skilled soldier but not even one bit boastful about his accomplishments even though in less than a year he had been accepted into an elite reconnaissance squad which meant that in the event of war he would be among the first to be dropped by parachute onto enemy territory to send information back to his officers. He was training for this every day while I sat in school feeling bored and lame. Joining the army for him was a ticket out of Savannah where he had been born and raised; a gorgeous beach boy raised on sand and surf with big, dangerous dreams.

Connor's greatest inspiration was his larger-than-life, first-generation German grandfather who had resisted the Third Reich and bled information to the United States that would have easily cost him his life during World War II. Connor was on a mission to make him proud, to serve his country, to do something worthy of his grandfather's approval. Enrolling in college was just not enough and he didn't feel that calling anyway. He could have been a scholar had he chosen that route I guess but he chose to put himself, his entire being, to task by joining the military.

He told me that he had no intention of getting into a relationship when he joined the army; in fact, he was on a completely different path. All he really wanted to do was jump out of planes and push his physical and mental limits. Now fate had thrown him an emotional curve-ball, and he had caught it. My response was to apologize for being a distraction. He accepted my apology and whispered in my ear, "Just promise you'll keep distracting me."

Connor would have already run ten miles with a thirty-pound equipment sack on his back in full uniform and steel-toed combat boots in the heat of a humid North Carolina summer morning before I would have even opened my eyes. Then, after a day of training to jump out of planes, ignoring the pain from the deep, penetrating blisters the thirty-pound sack had rubbed on both sides of his lower back, he would shower, dress casually – always his big high tops - and come find me.

I was too young and inexperienced to properly handle this kind of intense relationship. In contrast to Connor's overflowing affection, I would hold back, embarrassed, not knowing what to do or say. I was an unlikely, apologetic girlfriend. Anyone else would have given up but not him. He would laugh-off my inhibitions and work harder to break down my walls. What did I know of this kind of love, except for raw emotion which I was inclined to suppress? I had seen him enter the Judd Street house that first time, felt that first kiss, and had dreamed of him every night since. *That* was all I knew of this kind of love. Well, anyway, it felt right and I ached in those hours during eleventh grade, reading about star-crossed lovers but daydreaming about my own.

****

The phone rang on a random Tuesday night. "Hello?"

"Hey, Lucy. It's Connor. There's this party, well, ball thing I'm being forced to attend and it might actually be bearable if you come with me." That was Connor inviting me to a formal military ball that would take place on Friday night.

"Yes, of course, I'll go with you." I agreed with some secret hesitation. This was going to be our first official date apart from our meetings on Judd Street. Even though I was terrified of him asking me to dance and worried about my awkward personality malfunctioning in public around his fellow soldiers, I could not stop smiling.

The rest of the week was a speeding blur until the brakes slammed with me staring blankly into my meager closet. I had labored over what I should wear all week but kept pushing it to the back of my mind. Now, finally, I had to choose. There was actually only one item in my closet that seemed appropriate, a black velvet sundress that had a full skirt over black toile which made it appear kind of formal and gothic in honor of our meeting place (and Connor would never know I bought it from a thrift store). My black flats were shiny with a sleek, pointed toe. I topped it off with a pale pink sweater I found in my mom's cedar chest; one she used to wear in high school. I also wore her pearl necklace. My hair did its own thing which was to hang straight down to my shoulders. The only makeup I wore was cherry lip-gloss, careful not to overdo it.

Mary picked me up from home and delivered me to Judd Street where Connor soon arrived in his own red car this time... wearing a beret, an official-looking uniform, and the shiniest black shoes I had ever seen. I guess Andrew approved of our date since he was in tears at how beautiful we looked together, snapping pictures like he was my dad and I was going to prom or something. Pan was less thrilled. I wondered if he might have had a gothic-boy-likes-normal-girl crush by the way he glared at Connor and refused to even look at me.

My memory plays that night over like a magical fairytale. We sat at a large round table joined by some of his army buddies and their dates (who were all, incidentally, flaunting big breasts and plunging V-necks...I felt so juvenile in my 1960's pearl-studded sweater from my mom's cedar chest. Oh well.) Food was served and we ate while the soldiers talked about certain officers who regularly made their lives a living hell, finding great amusement in each other's comments especially as they related to the officers' wives whose necklines brushed their chins. Connor leaned over close to my ear and whispered, "Are you *sure* you don't want to slow dance with me? I'm an awesome dancer, you know, from all that practice I've been getting at Nevo." He was so irresistible and adorable and I was melting to his will by the moment. He didn't have to press too hard to squash my inhibitions about dancing...or anything for that matter. It wasn't long before he was leading me by the hand to the dance floor. I don't even remember the song; only how perfect he smelled and how strong his arms were, how perfectly pressed his uniform was, and how he squeezed my fingertips between his fingers.

At last, as if he had stayed an acceptable amount of time at this required event, we were on our way out of the Sheraton (and I had survived a social event without one regretful moment.) After a short drive, Connor parked his car in the lot behind the museum. I was thinking how I had never parked and made out with anyone before. Was it even legal? Honestly, at that point, I didn't really care.

Instead of reaching over to kiss me though, he jumped out of the car and was quick to open my door offering his hand to help me out. Okay, I was a little disappointed that my assumption about making-out had been wrong. In our town of urban sprawl, there were few places with any aesthetic appeal, but Connor had found this spot at the museum and thought it was appropriate for our next step. We walked along a path made of cobblestone leading us into a quiet, moonlit garden. A wooden bridge led the way to a gazebo near a few wrought iron benches. He lifted me as if a groom carrying his bride over a threshold and carried me to one of those benches surrounded by rose bushes covered in blossoms so fragrant in their last days. I sat while he knelt in front of me on one knee and held my hands between his like he liked to do. Connor cleared his throat and began, "Lucy, I know I'm nineteen, and this is going to sound a little weird, like elementary school, but I was hoping that, well, I was, umm, wondering if you will (clears throat again) be my girlfriend, I mean, you know, officially?" I glanced up to see the soft momentary glow of several fireflies flickering like my own iridescent light show against the darkness. I chuckled and raised my eyebrows at their apparent sign of approval. "Oh God, you must think this sounds so old..." But before he could utter the word "fashioned," I released him of his struggle.

Holding his gorgeous, blushing face, I said, "Connor, I feel like I already am your girlfriend. Since the first second I saw you walk into the house on Judd Street, I've felt a strange connection to you. I don't know what this is but it's pretty powerful and kind of scary and by the way, you are so cute right now. Of course, I will be your girlfriend -- officially."

It seemed like the time it took for his hand to reach up, slip under my hair and grasp the back of my neck was in slow motion. We were embraced in our first "official" kiss as Connor and Lucy. There would be many more kisses. Unfortunately, they would eventually be outnumbered by tears.

CHAPTER 9

The bell rang and he was sitting in his red Jetta parked in front of my school. I'm sure others watched with jealousy as I climbed into the car with that gorgeous man, well at least I secretly hoped they did. Who would have believed average Lucy Bells would have a boyfriend like this? I was just a quiet, nice girl who made good grades, ran track, and played the violin in the school's orchestra. I wasn't the track star or first chair violin; in fact, it was easy for apathy to set in with me, but Connor had taken over my priorities and there were no apathetic feelings there. I had fallen for him hard and the amount of time I spent with him, thinking of him, and talking to him on the phone was probably unhealthy for a young scholar on her way out of high school. Looking back now, I can see that I wasn't looking ahead, rather resting content in the present. I was enjoying the warm light that was radiating from my first and only love, and shining just for me.

Connor was the perfect boyfriend for me because he would not allow me to wallow in self-pity, at least in his presence. Trust me; he had his work cut out for him. I generally lived in the land of insecurity and doubt but especially when it came to my family. I never thought of myself as trailer park material, but that's where my family ended up after my dad's twenty-six years as a preacher abruptly came to an end.

Reverend Bobby Bells had been denying illness for about a decade. He had adult-onset diabetes that went unchecked and unmanaged. Maybe it was pure denial or just plain ignorance. A dozen or so cans of Mountain Dew every day, the appalling diet he kept, cheap cigars and zero exercise might have had something to do with it. He was our dad, our preacher, our 250 pounds of unhappy, sick man with an ironic rage living just below the surface. It still sounds weird to say that he was a preacher. My sister and I could never quite grasp why this cigar-smoking, foul-mouthed, abusive man would have chosen this profession. I suspect it was easy for him; it was just another lie. He was a true Dr. Jekyll and Mr. Hyde. The faces we had to put on just to sit through his sermons were like masks, vacant and emotionless.

During my dad's last days as a preacher, his sanity was checking out. Before the sickness took its toll, he had been an amazing actor. I mean he could curse my mom for all she was worth, hurl a fit of rage toward his wife and little girls, and then piously parade among his congregation. He could deliver a sermon so moving and heartfelt, so convincing and powerful that he really might have won an Academy Award. Each Sunday morning, our masks would come out and the wonderful Reverend and his wife and kids would be on stage for a couple of hours. "Don't miss this Sunday's performance of Preacher Bells and his family." That should have been on the church marquee instead of the choir director's clever play on letters: "What's missing in CH-CH? UR."

But now, his illness and heavy medication were diminishing

his ability to perform and his sermons were taking on a life of their own. These new sermons were like a window to his soul. They focused mostly on money and how no one was giving enough. He would accuse his congregation, "If you really believed in your *GOD*, you'd give this church more of your damned money instead of hoarding it to go on your precious shopping sprees and vacations. Now, damn it, this church needs more money (fist slams on the pulpit). It's damn near broke!" His eyes looked wild and crazy, but so did ours. Those plastic masks changed from vacant and emotionless to raised eyebrows over wide eyes, and mouths dropped open in disbelief. This had to be theatre, not real life. He was actually blowing his own cover, the very one his family had been forced to front for many years. Reverend Bells was cursing in the pulpit. He never did slip up and call out any of the "mullie-fuckers" he ranted about at home (it was years later that I learned the actual term for MF contained the word "mother").

This new lack of censorship infuriated the old southern church ladies and caused a few walk-outs. "I don't have to sit here and listen to this shit!" could be heard on their protest march down the aisle and out the front doors. I guess they had their own covers to blow.

Although I should have been under the pew with embarrassment, I sat right there through it all. I remember those moments like an out-of-body experience – like I was a spirit floating above my fleshy shell just observing it all; definitely theatre. Being ever rational, I could see both points of view. The church did need more money I guess, but shouldn't churchgoers hear a sermon, you know, something about forgiveness and salvation?

The church didn't tolerate my dad's ranting for very long.

"You have until February to vacate the parsonage. Our new minister and his family will be moving in come early March. I'm sorry Reverend." There was not much time to figure this one out considering it was the last week of January. I watched as Mr. Lambert delivered this message and left my father standing at the carport door, frozen and speechless for too many minutes; and yes, there would be hell to pay.

Being a preacher's family meant that we owned very few home furnishings. Each church provided a fully-furnished home for their preacher and his family, so my parents had never even owned their own couch. Pots, pans, and dishes were about all we had apart from our clothes. Just a step away from being homeless, we managed to get the church to set us up at the Traveler's Motor Lodge and Truck Stop on the outskirts of town until our next residence could be secured. I was excited about peanut butter and jelly sandwiches and canned soda every day for lunch and supper. And I finally had a swimming pool! My sister and I stood there, dwarfed by a dozen or so eighteen-wheelers, grasping the locked chain-link fence, watching the dirty, stagnant, frigid pool water. I looked up at Mary with adolescent excitement imagining what fun we could have. She looked back with teenage disappointment knowing there would be no fun. Besides being dirty, disgusting, and within peeping-tom range of chain-smoking, lonely truck drivers, it was the dead of winter and our pool was closed.

Our little motel room with two double beds was not meant for long-term living for a family of four, so my mother was finally getting a place of her own. She had chosen, with limited funds and a small loan from her parents, a single-wide trailer... fully furnished – perfect. There was a newly manufactured smell about the place, like hot glue and new carpet. I thought the interior decorator had done such a nice job coordinating all five rooms in different designs of light blue and pale pink plaid, stripe, and check. The carpet was pink shag.

The kitchen and living room took up about one-third of the trailer while the bedrooms and bathrooms took up the rest. I had the first and smallest room down the tiny hallway. Once inside, I would have to hang a sharp left to get around the single bed which was actually more like a cot. I could sit or stand in the space between my bed and dresser but that's about it. Mary's slightly larger room was just a few more steps down the narrow hallway. Then there was a bathroom, and finally my parents' bedroom which also contained a bathroom.

I admit it...I was embarrassed that I lived in a trailer. I just thought it meant something more than it did, like a metaphor for my future lack of accomplishment or something. Connor's love and acceptance attempted to prove me wrong. But anonymity was my best bet before I met him and I was great at that. Jr. High was quiet and solitary which fit nicely with my reclusive nature. This existence continued until Connor picked me out of the motley crowd on Judd Street.

I invited him to my home through embarrassed tears and sickening false pride. I didn't want my parents' trailer to define me. I had heard that judgmental phrase "trailer park trash" too many times in my life. I wondered if just living in a trailer caused one to fall under that category or if there was something more to it. I was also afraid that my dad's foul state of being might make Connor have second thoughts about developing our relationship.

Sitting in his car outside of my school I said, "I want you to come home with me, but first I have to tell you...I live in a trailer." I buried my face in my hands. It seems so sad, as I think back now, how much importance I placed on appearances. How could I have thought Judd Street was better? I guess it was a house; more dignified with its wooden slats and solid foundation. In contrast, the trailer was a quickly thrown together, rectangular box made of cheap metal, painted brown to look like wood, teetering on piles of cinder block. Did I mention it came with pink shag carpet?

Anyway, my pride was a coward in the face of Connor's unconditional love. He looked through every flaw I had and somehow came up with perfection. He just scoffed and then spoke in a sultry whisper, "You're perfect for me, Lucy Bells, and I love you. I don't care about your parents' trailer. But you do need to take me there so I can see where you sleep and dream about me." Then he started his car and revved the motor a little bit. After blowing-off my humiliation and crumbling my wall of shame, he pulled me in close for a gentle kiss proving he really did not care where I lived. Right there in his arms, in his car, I didn't have a care in the world.

Connor continued chipping away at my walls and agreed to meet me at The Record Exchange or on Judd Street until I was ready for him to see more. He was literally breaking apart my shell so I could emerge a confident, fearless woman. He did that for me and still loved me even when I refused to come out.

CHAPTER 10

I t had been a long afternoon at track practice running four miles through a path in the woods behind my school. The sun was slowly setting and I was hoping darkness would soon fall since I was about to take Connor to the trailer for the first time. No, I wasn't really ready, but what the hell. Maybe, in the darkness, it wouldn't be so bad. As soon as he saw me come out of the front doors of my school, he jumped out of his car and was quickly by my side. He took the heavy bookbag off my back and put it on his, grabbed my hand, and we were off. His favorite music group, New Order, was blasting "1963" which was typical but there were some obvious differences today: a pair of black snug-fitting cotton pants replaced his usual jeans, a gray body-hugging V-neck pullover that showed his muscular abdomen replaced his usual sweatshirt, and white canvas lace-up shoes replaced his big high tops. He smelled of cologne and looked so clean, so gorgeous. This was Connor getting ready to present himself to the parents of his future wife, his plans for which I was unaware.

In contrast, I felt dirty and underdressed beside him in my skimpy polyester track shorts, sweatshirt, and running shoes. "God, you really clean-up well in your civilian clothes. I feel like an ogre right now. Is all this for my mom and dad?" I said looking him up and down.

"All this (he paused as he rubbed his six-pack) is for you," and winked at me.

I smiled and had to quickly look away to keep him from seeing my red face and teary eyes. Who was this amazing person who had dropped into my meager existence? I didn't feel like I was enough for him. How could "all this" be for me? I was having a hard time imagining this gorgeous man arriving at the trailer park in Nowhereville, NC because he looked more like he should be walking into a New York City modeling agency. Leaving it up to me to give directions to the trailer was almost a mistake. I was tempted to lead him to the interstate and, going ninety miles per hour in his cherry-red Jetta, speed away from that town for some other fairytale life.

The long road leading up to the trailer park mocked me every day. Mimosa trees peaked from a forest of evergreens promising a tropical, floral delusion with the onset of spring. Further up, a tiny creek splashed along smooth weathered rocks. Thick Kudzu, though a parasitic nuisance, provided a lush, green valley of heart-shaped vegetation through which he drove us. I wondered if he noticed. As we emerged from the cool, shaded arbor, a handmade wooden fence paralleled the rest of the three-mile drive. Horses from the Diamond Springs Ranch galloped along the fencing or just stood still in their majesty. To me, it always seemed like they were looking down on us lowly trailer park dwellers. I mean, why not? They lived on a big ranch complete with stables, corrals, and a ranch house which always seemed more like a mansion.

About a quarter-mile up the road from the entrance that led to the ranch house, we took a left into the Freedom Manor Mobile Home Park. The tranquil drive leading up to my parents' trailer was too short. I needed about fifty more miles to prepare myself for what lay just a few feet ahead. Connor turned left and around the cul-de-sac to the corner lot with the brown trailer. "Here we are. Let's go," I said hurrying out of the car, trying to hide my hesitation, and feeling completely forsaken by the lingering sunlight. I wanted so badly to be the kid from the ranch; how impressive would that have been?

I thought I knew what waited for us inside; Dad sleeping in front of the TV while Mom washed dishes or something mundane like that. We were walking toward the door when Mom swung it open with a huge smile and a warm hug for Connor. It was a sweet beginning. What I thought would be a complete embarrassment proved not to be. My mom had cleaned and made her little piece of the world look nice and comfortable. She had also been cooking: steaming hot homemade biscuits, mashed potatoes, country fried steak and gravy, peas, and a chocolate sheet cake for dessert, complete with homemade sweet tea. The sheer excitement on Connor's face when he saw the table set for four was unforgettable and reminded me how sincere and unpretentious he was.

My mom had worked her southern hospitality to an extraordinary degree but it was my dad who shocked me the most. This was a man who was usually too drowsy and ill to even speak when I came home from school, but tonight was a different story. He actually stood up, wearing his best light blue, short-sleeved, button-up shirt with a red, white, and blue striped clip-on tie and shook hands with Connor. He said, "Well, I'm proud to have dinner with a real soldier tonight. Sit down and let's eat." Connor put my bookbag down and before I could even suggest that he take the tour, he had washed his hands at the kitchen sink, pulled up his sleeves, taken a seat beside my dad, and was pouring gravy all over his plate filled with my mom's delicious southern feast.

Tears welled up in my eyes when I saw how my parents welcomed Connor into their meager little home. "Come on, Lucy, sit down. I know you're hungry after that long track practice." "Yes, I am, Mom. This looks amazing." I bounced a glance of gratitude her way and she could see the relief in my eyes. I felt guilty about saying to her just hours before on our way to school that I was embarrassed to bring Connor home because I lived in "a metal box." How cruel and thoughtless I had been, shallow and ungrateful, considering how much more than just metal it was right now. It was a home that actually embraced and loved Connor.

Over dinner, Connor openly talked about his home in Savannah, his family, and his job making it clear that he could not tell everything about his recon unit. Everything he said just elevated his coolness in my eyes. He complimented the food almost too many times and laughed at my dad's colloquialisms such as "fittin' to eat" and his terrible, borderline perverted jokes. I think he temporarily unearthed a civilized part of my dad that seemed to have been suppressed many hard years ago as they discussed President Bush, the army, and the growing conflict in the Middle East. My dad had become a CNN junkie and was delighted to have someone listen to his interpretations of the anchors' reports since he was hard-pressed to find an audience in my mom or me. It was here that Dad earned the affectionate nickname "Mr. B." Connor found him to be entertaining and lovable but that was only because he brought out the one flicker of goodness that lingered in his bitter, sick, demented little heart.

After we ate, Connor and I cleared the table. "Mrs. Bells, you go sit down now. We've got this. You've already been in here cooking all afternoon. I'm washin' and she's dryin'." He winked at me as he handed me the "dryin'" towel. This was actually fun. I couldn't imagine this evening being any better – even at the ranch house. I was seeing what an amazing person Connor was. He had deep-seated politeness, was honest, open, funny, and accepting. He also possessed the ability to bring out the best in a crazy old man.

When the dishes were washed, dried, and put away, Connor thanked Mom again for the delicious meal. Dad had already retired to his chair in front of the television and dropped off into a food and medication-induced coma. I took Connor's hand and led him down the hallway to my room. "So this is it," I whispered through a sigh, shrugging my shoulders as I turned on a small lamp. He quietly closed the door behind him, and standing in the small space between my bed and the wall lined with a dresser and a bookcase, he pulled me tight to his body and kissed me. What a rush, knowing my parents were steps away in the next room. It didn't matter. I desired to be nowhere else on earth than in that tiny space filled with us.

We sat on my little bed and talked about what homework I had to do and my small record collection. He leaned back against the wall and moaned while rubbing his tight stomach, then lifted his shirt and exposed his perfectly formed abs.

"Wow, Connor, you shouldn't...just pull your shirt down," I said, embarrassed.

"Why? You know you like it," he said, picking on my pru-

46

dence. He sat up, hugged me, and said, "I have loved everything about tonight, Lucy Bells. Thank you for trusting me enough to bring me here. I just hope your parents don't get sick of me being here all the time."

"I wouldn't worry about that. You're the only person my dad has shown any civility to in a long time."

"He's awesome," Connor said with a little chuckle.

He soon left for the base taking with him a trio of hearts belonging to my parents and me. In Connor's absence I merely survived, only truly feeling alive in his presence.

CHAPTER 11

I reached over to rub the blonde stubble on the back of his head. I loved the way it felt when it had grown out a little. He looked at me with those green eyes and smiled a sheepish grin and I knew then how this had happened; it was his God-given charm. He was irresistible and my parents had fallen for it almost as hard as I had. It was Friday afternoon and I was on my way to Washington D.C. with Connor for a surprise birthday weekend. Since I was turning seventeen the next day, maybe my parents thought I was old enough to go or maybe they just couldn't say "no" to Connor. "I still can't believe my parents said this trip was ok. They hardly know you."

"Don't worry. They totally trust me," Connor assured.

"Yeah, but why should they? Why should I?" I said trying to fake some kind of concern. I received "the look" - one eyebrow raised. "You know I'm just kidding, Connor. This is the best birthday I've ever had. I can't wait to get there."

I was already thinking about what might happen overnight, and I was ready. I tried not to freak myself out about it, but it was kind of a big deal. I was on an overnight trip with my boyfriend of almost three months and not just for one night, but two. He had waited for me and never pushed our intimacy too far, but I felt so close to him already; it felt like the right time and God knows, I wanted him. It was around 9:00pm when Connor checked us into a Holiday Inn Express on the outskirts of D.C. We had our fast food drive-thru dinner which we scarfed down sitting indian style across from each other on the bed. Much to my dismay, Connor was yawning and seemed tired after eating his food. The TV was on...the only light – flickering with some old black and white movie; volume too low to hear. It was not long before he was sound asleep. Honestly, I was disappointed and trying not to take it too personally. But then I began to think about what his day must have been like: up by 4:30am for physical training, working and training all day, and then making the five-hour drive to D.C. for my birthday. I spooned behind him and fell asleep, loving his inner and outer strength and falling ever-deeper in love with him.

I woke up to the sound of Connor coming into the hotel room. "Good morning," I said, sitting up, finger brushing my hair.

"I thought my birthday girl should have breakfast in bed," placing three McDonald's bags on the bed in front of me. With that remark, he kissed me, and then again and held it for a moment. "Happy Birthday, Baby."

"Thank you. This whole thing...this whole trip is so amazing. I'm so happy to be here with you."

He replied, "You're welcome, and me too."

After breakfast, I got ready and we were off to see the sights of our nation's Capital. It was my first visit to D.C. and I was amazed by what I saw. We walked along the Mall and visited the Washinton, Lincoln, and Jefferson Memorials, and the Smithsonian. It was a typical cold and windy January weekend, so we held each other close as we walked. Connor squeezed my fingertips between his fingers like a nervous habit. I loved it. We must have been glowing as it seemed everyone who passed us stared, smiled, approved. Maybe it was just my imagination but we stood out like our union was something ordained...supposed to be.

After we walked along the Vietnam Memorial and watched the Changing of the Guard at the Tomb of the Unknown Soldier, it was time to call it a day. But first, we stopped in a little bakery where Connor ordered two vanilla cupcakes with buttercream icing; one lit candle to be placed in mine. He set the cupcakes down on our tiny round table and said for me to make a wish. That was easy. I closed my eyes and thought, "I wish for Connor and Lucy to last forever." I opened my eyes and blew out the candle. "So, do I get to know what you've wished for?"

"You know I can't tell you. I want this one to come true." I think back on this particular moment with a healthy amount of disdain for whatever entity grants birthday wishes so one-sidedly. Connor and Lucy would definitely last forever, but only for me.

We headed back to the hotel room after eating our cupcakes. Connor wasn't talking as much as he usually did. He seemed more serious, quiet, and focused. I thought maybe The Wall or The Tomb had gotten to him. I grabbed my nightshirt and headed straight for the shower as soon as I entered the room. After being cold all day, the hot water thawed my bones and relaxed my tense muscles. I probably stayed in there too long since the air was thick like fog when I pulled back the shower curtain.

While I was drying off, the bathroom door opened and then there was darkness. Connor took the towel from me without a word and gently dried my back and my hair. Then he let the towel drop to the floor. He picked me up and carried me to the bed. Still no words.

I felt the crisp, cold sheet below me and then the heat from his soft skin and the full pressure of his body on mine. My heart was beating so hard, not fast, just hard and steady. I knew he could feel it. I transcended, with one gentle kiss followed by breathy whispers into my ear concerning my well-being, "Are you okay? Is this too much? Is this okay? Sure you're fine, Lucy? You can't imagine how much I love you." This is how it should be... perfect. Forehead to forehead, tears ran down both our faces mingling in splotches on the pillow. He held me close to him, almost too tightly, for the rest of the night.

I woke first the next morning feeling different, closer to him, a little older...sore. Connor was fully asleep, relaxed and just dead weight with his arm and leg over me. I wiggled my way around to face him and whispered, "Good morning," in his ear and kissed the soft hot skin around his neck. He responded by pulling me on top of him in one motion. He kissed me, smiled, and finally said, "Good morning, Beautiful."

We were on the road well before check-out. I reached over and rubbed his stubble again. In just seventeen short years I had already found the love of my life.

CHAPTER 12

There was no more need for Judd Street as it had served its purpose by being a portal that had successfully brought us together. Anyway, Connor was satisfied to spend his free time with me at home, in the trailer, talking and laughing with my dad while I did my homework. A week before spring break, I let my parents know that Connor wanted to take me to Savannah to meet his family. I thought at some point they might question me about spending so many nights with Connor, alone. Neither one of them ever did. In fact, after a short talk behind a closed bedroom door, they offered their car since it was bigger and would be more comfortable for the long trip. They could just use the station wagon for the weekend if they needed to go anywhere. I think it's safe to say my parents trusted Connor.

Early on Saturday morning, Mom got up and cooked bacon, eggs, and biscuits for breakfast. It was her idea to have Connor go ahead and spend the night so that we could get an early start on our trip. We were well-fed and on our way before eight o'clock.

I finally felt nervous when we turned on the dirt road that led to his parents' house. Doubt - what if they don't like me? Fear - what if they don't think I'm good enough for their son? I was taking in the huge yard, the big brick house, the swimming pool..."Good God, what's wrong, Lucy?" Connor asked with a detectable amount of concern in his voice. I guess the expression on my face was giving me away.

"I'm scared to meet your family. I just hope they like me," I blurted out.

"They will love you, trust me. And if for some strange reason they don't, to hell with them, ok? It's you and me now. So, where is that beautiful smile?" Connor refused to give my self-loathing a leg to stand on. He loved me and that was really all that mattered.

When I first laid eyes on Trudi, I saw where Connor got his good looks and German genes. She was a gorgeous blonde with a strong, healthy build. Her green eyes were focused on one thing, her beautiful boy. She is, perhaps, the one person on earth who loves him more than me. I was an afterthought following their long embrace. "Oh, hi darlin'. We are so happy to meet you," she said with a thick southern accent.

Mr. Hawthorn scared me. He shook Connor's hand and said, "Welcome home, son. Where the hell's your car and who does this one belong to?" "Lucy's parents let us use their car because it's bigger or whatever. Dad, this is Lucy."

"Uh-huh. I'll see y'all inside."

"He's just like that so let it go," Connor said. Excellent advice. Mr. Hawthorn continued down the hill in the backyard that led to a garage. He spent the majority of his time tinkering with his cars and motorcycles. He was as disinterested in me as he could be.

I spent the next two days in coastal Georgia soaking up the sun and all that I could about Connor and his family. By the time I woke up on the first morning, Connor had been running, showered, and had breakfast and coffee with his mother on the back porch. This was a Saturday morning, and yet they all seemed so disciplined and busy. After I ate breakfast, Connor took me on a walking tour of their property. We walked down a dirt road holding hands for a while until we came to a stream. A tire swing was still hanging from a large tree branch faithfully waiting for someone to jump off into the water. He showed me the rope burn scar on the underside of his upper right arm from playing too rough when he was a kid. We walked down the hill in their backyard past the garage where his father, who didn't even glance our way, was busy working. He just didn't want to be bothered. We visited the kennels where Trudi kept her rescue animals until they were healthy enough to be adopted.

During the evening, Connor patiently taught me how to play chess sitting by the fireplace and reluctantly walked me through photo albums of his school days; mostly of him in different sports uniforms. Beyond those pictures, I did not soak up much more of his history. I asked Connor to show me pictures of his old girlfriends but he only commented, "What old girlfriends?"

Connor's family was not an open book so I came away knowing only these things for sure: his mother worshiped him-her only child, his dad was scary, there was more than meets the eye. I just assumed it was my oversight or nervous self-consciousness that had caused me to come away so unenlightened. They seemed to love me though; a shy, soft-spoken, southern girl. There was something special about us together and it was undeniable. Those were the best days of my life.

CHAPTER 13

The mountains of North Carolina are a special place. They don't flaunt the high, jagged peaks of the Rockies or the Cascades. They have lived beyond those first two hundred million years and are more refined, rounded, and weathered with geology and history; a perfect stage for this milestone in our relationship. We were young lovers speeding around the curves on a skinny two-way road, hugging the side of a Blue Ridge cliff.

My junior year in high school had finally come to an end and I had managed straight A's, long-distance track meets, numerous orchestra performances, a part-time job, and my first boyfriend with ease. Connor and I were off again on another trip to celebrate my freedom. This one was even more important to him than taking me to Savannah to see his home, where he grew up, and meet his parents. I was up for the challenge though: Grandfather Herrmann, "Warrior."

The mountain retreat where his grandparents spent part of the year was a hidden jewel nestled deep in a tall stand of cedars and pines with a rocky river flowing along its border. Connor pulled into the lot and parked his car. "We're here." He reached over and put his hand on my left knee. I reached down and took his hand in mine.

"What's wrong, Connor? You seem more nervous than me this time."

"Lucy, I can't explain how much this means to me, you know, for you to meet my grandfather." My grip on his hand tightened and then I kissed his fingers. It was sinking in how much he admired and loved this man. Thankfully, the trip to meet his parents had made me more confident for this one.

"Well, I cannot wait to meet him," I said with an easy, excited tone. Connor looked at me with childlike embarrassment for being so emotional which I found to be utterly vulnerable and purely irresistible. After a soft kiss on his pouty closed lips, I whispered, "Let's go."

Our visit began in a restaurant modeled after a ski lodge. There was a very large fireplace and everything was rustic, wooden, and perfectly themed. We were escorted to a table situated by a huge window. As we approached, Connor's grandparents stood up to welcome us. Grandfather Herrmann fit the phrase "larger-than-life." He was tall and intimidating. I could see why it was such a big deal to impress him. He just looked important, like his existence was essential in the history of the world. Seriously. Connor was smiling. Thank God. He reached out to shake his grandfather's hand but was grabbed up for a bear hug like a little kid. I smiled at seeing this vulnerable side of my soldier.

"Welcome, Grandson. You are looking well." Mr. Herrmann still spoke with a heavy German accent and deep commanding voice. "Sit here and tell us about your life at this time and don't leave out a detail. But first, we must become acquainted with this young lady you have at your side." I blushed as he took my hand between both of his just like Connor had done before.

"This is Lucy. She has agreed to spend some of her free time with me and as you can see, I am very, very lucky." Connor was smiling and looking straight at me as he said this.

"Indeed, Grandson. She appears to be a jewel, but we cannot judge her solely on this." He winked at me and smiled. Grandmother Herrmann scooted closer to me and rubbed a couple of circles on my back hoping to help me feel more at ease.

"Well, Miss Lucy Bells plays the violin, she runs track, she makes honor roll. She is way beyond my station, Grandfather. The best thing I've done in a while."

Over an Italian feast already chosen for us, the conversation turned to the beautiful surroundings, the perfect timing of our visit, and the trouble in the Middle East. I quickly realized I was too uneducated about current events to keep up with the flow (secretly wishing I had spent a little more time watching Wolf with my dad.) After dessert, Mrs. Herrmann and I took our leave to have a "nice walk home." She hooked her left arm around my right elbow like we were old friends. We slowly passed the swimming pool, the golf course entry, a beautifully ornate gazebo strung with tiny white lights, and finally arrived at their condo.

Upon entering, she walked straight to the fireplace while I sat on a stool at the bar that separated the living room and kitchen. "It gets chilly in here at night for the old folks...old bones – close to the skin," she said, explaining why she was lighting a fire in June. Then she walked over to the kitchen and began brewing a pot of coffee. "You know, I am not Connor's grandmother by blood, although it seems that I am. I am the only mother Trudi has ever known but I am not her birth mother."

"Yes, I figured as much. She is so blonde and green-eyed and you have such a dark complexion." Mrs. Herrmann's hair was gray, coarse, bone straight, and hung down to her mid-back. Her cheekbones were high and defined; her eyes, dark brown.

"I am Native American, full-blooded Cherokee. I married Mr. Herrmann after he defected to the United States during Hitler's War. I was well into marrying age by that time and to be honest, my family already considered me an old maid at twenty-three," she laughed. "Can you believe that?"

"No. That's way too young to be an old maid," I agreed.

"Trudi had to leave her mother at a very young age, just a baby, really. She was quite sick; very ill with cancer and unable to travel with the family. Mr. Herrmann had to make a dreadful decision for his family and left her there to die in Nazi Germany. She was in a hospital, near death, when he and his girls had to leave but there is no account of her final days. We just don't know exactly what happened to her although the tiny town was eventually destroyed."

"Connor never told me this story."

"Well, Mr. Herrmann made the difficult choice to look ahead and not behind. We never did look back; spent not a moment on regret. We raised his girls in a loving family. I have loved them as my own. I've never given birth to my own child. The girls have been my life since I was twenty three years old."

She had been staring across the living room into the fireplace for the last few seconds as if she was lost in a distant land. Now her gaze turned upon me. "Are you alright, dear? How about a cup of coffee?" Maybe she noticed the look of anguish on my face.

"Yes ma'am. That would be great." At least I was hoping it would be great since that would be my first cup of coffee ever.

"Why did Mr. Herrmann have to leave Germany so quickly?" I asked as she made her way into the kitchen.

"It was a matter of life or death. He had to leave at that instant or face his own death for treason. Though he wore a Nazi uniform, he was not a Nazi. He was a spy, dear. But that's about all I know. Is this how you like your coffee?" It was tan and still swirling around in the dainty china cup teetering on a matching saucer.

"Yes ma'am. It looks... delicious." I could tell that was the end of that conversation.

Seeing Connor walk through the door was breathtaking. He had worn khakis and a black polo to see his grandparents. His hair was freshly buzzed and his face was suntanned. But those green eyes...I had never seen him so relaxed and happy. He and his Grandfather stayed behind at the lodge for a night cap of bourbon. I could smell it and taste it when he walked right over to me and lightly kissed my lips. We all sat in the living room and listened as Grandfather Herrmann entertained us with stories about Connor's mother when she was a teenager dating for the first time; afraid to bring anyone home to meet him for fear of interrogation. He laughed at the idea of young men fearing him. Surely he could understand why.

Later on, after his grandparents went to bed, Connor and I sat together on the couch. "So, what do you think of my grandparents?"

"I think they are wonderful. I can see why you love and admire your grandfather so much," I said.

"Yes. I do. His opinion means more to me than anyone else's. I needed to talk to him about something very important." He scooted over closer to me and took both of my hands in his. I was actually afraid of what he was about to say. "My grand-father really likes you. You are the only girl I have ever even considered bringing to meet him. He said you have 'substance'." Connor made air quotes with his fingers.

"Well, substance is good," I replied with a smug, crooked smile feeling relieved.

"Yes, it's very good. Maaaan...I'm not used to liquor," Connor said rubbing his head. "Two shots and I'm spent." We laughed about his low tolerance. I wanted to ask him about his real grandmother but I didn't think it was the right time. We soon kissed goodnight. He slept on the couch and I slept in the guest room. There would be no sneaking around the German spy.

I woke up to the sweetest vision. Connor was sitting on the side of my bed, smiling. "What?" I said protesting to him watch-ing me sleep. "Come on and have some breakfast, Sleeping Beauty." The four of us drank coffee and ate croissants with but-ter and strawberry preserves on the balcony. Only out of polite-ness, he invited me to go golfing with him and his grandfather. I wished the two of them a wonderful day but declined to go, choosing instead to spend the morning with Grandmother Her-rmann shopping at the farmer's market and preparing a picnic lunch for the four of us.

We packed ingredients for fresh tomato sandwiches with mayo, salt and pepper, ambrosia fruit salad, and a blueberry muffin for each of us. "Now we can't forget these," she said with a wink as she carefully packed four champagne chutes, a mason jar of freshly squeezed orange juice, and an unopened bottle of champagne. "We can't have a picnic without a proper mimosa toast."

"Sounds great," I said, having no idea what a mimosa was.

She drove us in one of their golf carts to the picnic area where we set the table with a red and white checkered tablecloth and the rest of the food and drinks. When the men arrived in another golf cart, Mr. Herrmann dramatically grabbed his wife and carefully dipped her back, only a little, and planted a kiss right on her lips. "Oh, Edmund, behave around the young ones," she said, blushing and chuckling. Connor was looking on in complete admiration and awe.

"Oh well, I must teach my grandson how to keep the lady around," he joked. We all laughed.

"That's us in fifty years, right?" Connor quietly asked me.

"Most definitely," I said grabbing his arm and laying my head on his big bicep.

Grandmother Herrmann began our picnic with a mimosa toast: "To long-lasting love affairs."

"If only with you, my dear lady," said Grandfather Herrmann. "If only with you."

Connor and I raised our glasses to meet theirs and I was sure we had this one in the bag.

By the time evening fell, we felt nature pulling us outside. We stole away from the condo just in time to see the sun's fading rays paint the clouds fifty different shades of orange and red outlining them in silver against a baby blue canvas sky. At twilight, when the sky was navy and the stars were just flickering into view, we held hands and ran barefoot on the cold smooth rocks that dotted and disrupted the flow of the rushing water. After several minutes of running past tall pines, we came upon a clearing of lush green grass where we fell on our backs and watched the magnificent star show. Connor took my hand and held it up outlining constellations with my finger... "And right over here is the Big Dipper. You see, the handle is bent and the cup is here."

"I see. It's beautiful." We just lay there holding hands watching as the sky filled with more stars than I had ever seen. Connor eventually turned on his side to face me and began to gently stroke my cheek, then my chin, my neck, my chest. He watched his fingers as they toyed with the buttons on my shirt. A tear rolled down his cheek. "What's wrong?" I asked.

"Oh. You saw that?" he said, embarrassed. "Nothing really. It's just my grandparents. They're so old, you know. And... maybe I'm just a little afraid that I love you too much already."

We held each other on that little spot of grass in the darkness under the shimmering black velvet sky. I, too, was afraid this was too perfect so I held on tighter. I didn't ask Connor about his real grandmother, and it never even occurred to me to wonder if he possessed his grandfather's ability to look ahead with no regrets; to not look back. I would find out soon enough.

******

The smell of coffee and bacon woke me out of a sound sleep. I crept out of my room and found Connor busy in the kitchen scrambling eggs, frying bacon, and making toast for breakfast while his grandparents were outside on the balcony getting the table set. "Good morning," I said as I wrapped my arms around him from behind. "Cute apron." He was wearing his grandmother's ruffled, flowered one.

He turned around for a quick kiss and then started giving orders: "Can you get the butter and cream from the fridge? Oh, and will you take the orange juice outside?" "Sure," I said laughing at him in chef mode.

We ate Connor's delicious breakfast and had light conversation about the beautiful weather and plans for summer. Mrs. Herrmann expressed her wish for us to visit again very soon. Mr. Herrmann protested, "Ah, these young kids have better things to do than lounge around with old geezers like us, dear." Connor and I both said, "No, we don't." We all laughed. Not long after that, we said our goodbyes and drove away from their little piece of paradise. They stood there holding hands, waving until we were out of sight. That was the last time Connor would ever see his hero, his grandfather, the warrior.

CHAPTER 14

Summer vacation should have given us more hours to be together, and possibly more time to spend in the mountains, but the army didn't see it that way. Trouble was brewing in the Middle East and Connor's training intensified. My dad's obsession with Wolf Blitzer also intensified and for once we shared an interest. I was just waiting to hear that a war had started; then I could officially break down and slip into that deep, dark place I already felt lurking behind me.

The word came at the most bizarre time. My parents had chosen a seafood restaurant for dinner that was more than a few miles away; out of town, in the country. We drove down miles and miles of two-lane roads to get plates piled high with fried seafood and sweet tea from mason jars. A television mounted in the corner changed from "Jeopardy" to a "Special Report." The noisy restaurant hushed, the TV volume rose, my stomach felt sick, my parents looked worried. We sat at our four-top hearing the news that Iraq had invaded Kuwait. With an unprecedented urgency, we left food on our plates, money on the table, and headed for the door.

Not a word was spoken on the long drive home, at least not one that I remember. We sat together in our little den and watched CNN for hours. I tried to reach Connor by calling the barracks but no one answered. Finally, three long days and endless nights later, our phone rang. Connor tried to convey a sense of calm, but I could hear the urgency in his voice, "Hey Babe. Look, I need you to come see me at the base."

"What's going on? Can you just tell me now?"

"Just come to my barracks. I need to see you and your mom and dad. Try to come soon, okay?"

"Mom, Dad, Connor needs to see us at the base."

He was waiting for us on the sidewalk so Mom pulled the car right up to the curb. I ran to him and jumped into his arms. Despite the occasion, he tried to be upbeat and give off a nonchalant air. "Heeyyy! How's my favorite girl? Huh? It's ok." I couldn't manage one word. "We're deploying in the next couple of days to go...somewhere...and I can't leave the base. I want you to know that I will call you every single chance I get and then I want you to inform my mom and dad. Don't worry, ok?" Now he was holding my face on both sides so that he could look directly at me. "Listen up...it's ok." I couldn't speak and my body was already doing that weird jerking thing that happens when you try to hold back tears. "You'll be alright. You've got to take care of Mr. B. He's going to worry himself sick until I get back." He was just trying to lighten the mood even though it was true.

"Connor, we love you, son. Be safe now and come back home to us. You know I'll be watching Wolf." My dad was a different man when it came to Connor. Mom was trying not to cry but tears were streaming anyway. We each hugged him tightly. I managed, "I love you," placed my closed lips on his for a moment, and then we had to leave. Mom drove home while I sat in the back, bent over, burying my face in my hands, numb to the world.

I was used to being alone. That was my thing, isolated loner. But Connor Hawthorn had changed all that. I had never really considered myself lonely until Connor wasn't there anymore. Now I was not just alone; there was an empty space where he would be, a hand I couldn't hold, a voice I couldn't hear, a car not waiting for me by the curb.

My parents and I sat in the living room watching Wolf Blitzer for hours. The journalists were embedded in Kuwait, reporting from the front lines. The television screen was awash with the color of sand. What strange comfort I found in watching the war unfold in real-time; in turning on the TV and seeing where he was. I watched naively thinking one of those reporters might interview Connor or just maybe he would walk by, but he was busy with the business of waiting for war. I, too, would have to wait it out. I waited for his return for nine months.

My lonely summer came to an end after weeks of watching the news and working at The Record Exchange. I started my senior year of high school and tried to care about it. I was lonely, sad, worried, and preoccupied with Connor's mortality.

The letters started to come about two months after he left.

Dear Lucy,

I'm sitting in the damn sand right now waiting for something, anything to happen. I have sand in my ears, my eyes, my nose, my hair, my ass...you name it. I'm doing pretty well though. Bunking with about twelve guys and missing you insanely. Please know that I'm going to be alright. I am coming home so don't worry about that. Hell or high water couldn't keep me from you. I wish I was sitting outside of your school waiting to see you come out of those glass doors. You can't imagine how it makes me feel to know you are wait-

ing for me. I love you. I love your family. I love you and me together. Mrs. Hawthorn…just trying that on. I like it a lot. More later. Gotta go. Training is endless and it helps the time go by. Love C

****

Dear Lucy,

I keep waiting for something to happen but it just doesn't. Nothing to recon after all that training. A couple of my buddies and I broke rank last night and hopped on the back of a beat-up pickup that some Kuwaiti man was driving past our base. They love us here. It's like we are famous. They took us deep into their village. I couldn't have found my way out by myself if Jesus himself was calling me. You can't imagine how dark it gets when the sun goes down in the desert. Anyway, I finally had some real Middle-Eastern food. My buddies and I were invited into their little house, filled up with kids of all ages. There was a round table close to the ground filled with food and we all sat on the floor around it and ate until we were sick. They just kept bringing food out to us and saying, "Thank you, American soldiers." They were so sweet. I felt like a teenager sneaking out at night. We could have been in some deep shit but the man brought us right back to the gate where he picked us up. No one even knew. Well, not much else has been going on. I have been working on my biceps. I know you like that. Right now I've got to go find somebody with a fan because it's hotter than the gates of hell. Love and miss you. C

His letters were my life support. I survived by the words he wrote to me, reading them, over and over, holding them in my hands as a temporary replacement for him. I collected them like they were valuable artifacts; smelled the paper hoping in vain to get a whiff of his scent, desperate for nostalgia. They came in bundles, carelessly shoved in the mailbox. I would be missing for hours unwilling to share a word he wrote until I could speak them without crying.

Dear Lucy

I miss you. These words don't really do justice for what I'm feeling. Last year around this time we were in Washington celebrating your birthday. Sorry I'm not there with you today to begin your 18th year the right way. I would rub my hands over your warm skin and run my fingers through your soft hair. God, Lucy, you just don't know how badly I miss you. I miss your voice, your hair brushing my face, the color of your eyes, your small, soft hands, your body, your scent. This separation is killing me. Sometimes I wonder how it would be if I hadn't met you and fallen in love with you. How would this experience be affecting me if I didn't have you waiting for me to come home to? You have changed me. I am not my own anymore; I am yours. I hope you'll forgive me for being so dramatic. I'm in my bunk right now imagining you right here. I am just short of desperate. Here's a tear…it's for you. Happy Birthday, baby. Until I see you again.

Connor Hawthorn

Some of his letters could not be shared no matter my emotional state. I lived and breathed his words. If nothing else, they were proof that I was loved, that I was enough, that I was more than just a girl alone in her tiny trailer park room.

"Lucy, come to the phone!" Mom yelled from the living room. I tore out of my room thinking it was Connor, but it wasn't. It was Trudi. She was calling to deliver the devastating news: "Hi, darlin'. I just wanted to let you know that Grandfather Herrmann suffered a massive heart attack and passed away this morning." I was speechless of course. "We don't want to tell Connor while he's in Saudi Arabia. It would just upset him too

68

much."

"Oh, I'm so sorry," I finally managed though broken vocals. "Connor is going to be..."

"Please don't mention it in letters or if he happens to call, ok? He's got to be focused over there and this would just tear him up."

"I know. I won't mention it. I'm so sorry. How is Mrs. Herrmann?"

"Mama is staying with us for a little while until she is feeling better. She's very sad but she is doing as good as can be expected."

What a wicked turn of events. My heart broke for Connor.

CHAPTER 15

The flame was too hot to survive. I shouldn't have been feeling this way about anyone so quickly, so early, or so young. I was barreling toward my own fickle demise. But before the fall, we loved again. He found his way through the desert sand and back home to me. Nine months of loneliness ended with a late night phone call. "Hello?" I said after dashing to the phone straight out of a deep sleep.

"Hey baby. Guess what. I'll be home in two days."

"Connor!??!"

"It's so great to hear your voice right now. Just come to the base on Saturday morning and there will be people to guide you to the landing field. I gotta go now. Sorry this is so short. I love you."

"I love you too." That was all I could say before the phone call ended. I was frozen with conflicting emotions: excitement and dread. I would soon see Connor's face and feel his kiss again; he was coming home safe and unharmed. He would soon learn about his grandfather's death; that his hero was gone.

Plans were made and Connor's family was coming to North Carolina for his homecoming. This made me nervous. Here we go again with the trailer. I wondered if Connor had told them. How could I be worrying about that when I was about to see Connor in less than twenty-four hours? I was selfish and jealous. I just wanted him to myself. In spite of that, there was going to be a crowd waiting for him to get off that big, gray army plane: his parents, my parents, my sister – well it seemed like a crowd. When the Hawthorns arrived from Savannah, my parents, Mary, and I welcomed them to our corner lot in the mobile home park. Embarrassment is overrated so I had to let my trailer-shame go. Anyway, they seemed like they couldn't care less. They ate hotdogs and hamburgers from the grill and drank sweet tea from Dixie cups. Mr. Hawthorn and Dad talked war over the grill while Trudi and Mom kept looking over at me and smiling...coyly. Yes, it felt weird. Mary and I made big poster board signs saying, "WELCOME HOME CONNOR!" I really just wanted it to be over so Connor and I could get back to our old routines.

"Well, Joan, Honey, I really love your cozy home. It's decorated so nicely."

Humble as ever, my mom replied with a chuckle, "I know it's not much...but it's ours. Lucy has told me all about y'all's beautiful home."

"Yes, well, I know Mr. Bells isn't in the best health but I do wish you all could come for a visit."

"Well now, Bobby Bells loves to ride. He's not too bad off for that." They laughed together. Mom brought up the topic of Mr. Herrmann's passing so that she could personally offer her condolences. Trudi thanked her for the thoughtful card.

"I'm so worried about telling Connor. I hope he doesn't take it too hard."

"I know they were very close. Lucy told me about how much Connor loved his grandfather. I am so sorry he has to come home to that news."

Mr. Hawthorn and Dad never did come inside. They talked by the grill, checked out the riding lawn mower Connor would sometimes use, and looked over at the Diamond Springs Ranch, pointing and motioning in that direction. Trudi said it was time to go back to the motel so they could get a good night's sleep. Connor was supposed to arrive some time the next morning so we wanted to get there as early as the base would allow. We hugged and said goodbye like old friends.

I was happy that Mary was spending the night with us. She never did that anymore since she moved to Judd Street. We helped Mom with what was left to clean up while Dad retired to his chair. After they went to bed, we stayed up late. I was too excited and filled with anxiety to sleep. We talked about Judd Street. I secretly missed my corner chair. I missed Pan and his journal. I missed Andrew fussing over me. I wondered but didn't ask if Judd Street missed me back.

I woke everyone up around 5am taking a shower. I could smell bacon frying and coffee brewing when I left the bathroom several minutes later. I came to the kitchen with my robe on and hair wrapped up in a towel. "Hey Mom, will you pour me a cup of coffee and put some cream in it, please?" The smell was nostalgic taking me back to the mountain retreat with Connor's grandparents. "Since when do you like coffee, Lucy?"

"It's kind of a long story," I began. Then I told Mom about Connor's real grandmother and how she was left dying in Germany during the war. "And then he found the current Mrs. Herrmann and they raised the girls together. Now finally for the part about coffee...after her story, she handed me a beautiful china cup and saucer with coffee, sugar and cream in it, I drank it, and actually thought it was delicious."

"That's some story. It must have been awful for them, leaving their mother and his wife like that."

"Well, I'm sure it was but she said Mr. Herrmann never looked back or had any regrets. It was like they just found each other and sort of lived happily ever after I guess."

"Well, it's a blessing to be able to accept what life deals you without dwelling too much on the bad parts," Mom said most likely reflecting on her own life while unknowingly giving her daughter some of the most important advice she would ever receive.

"Yeah, I guess," I said.

I jumped up and hurried to my room because reality hit me; in just a few hours I was going to be face to face with Connor Hawthorn. I had to get ready: white sundress, sandals, hair loose because that's how he liked it. Mom, Dad, Mary, and I were packed in the car by 7am with our "Welcome Home" signs.

We met up with Connor's family on base. They beat us there by a few minutes but we were still among the first people at the landing field for the big homecoming. Over the next hour, more and more families arrived; children, wives, mothers, fathers, girlfriends. Our collective gaze was toward the wide-open Carolina blue sky where American flags were waving above our heads. Eventually, a grey dot, and another, and another appeared out of nowhere. Screams and cheers spread through the crowd. They were planes bringing our soldiers home. One of them contained Connor. He was up there, about to land. That sickening masochist who lives in my head was trying to ruin this for me: "What if he's changed? What if he doesn't love you anymore? What if he ignores you?" Her "What if" questions were brutal but thankfully today, she was the one being ignored. Her questions fell flat. My knees were already shaking.

The planes landed and eventually after what seemed an eternity, soldiers emerged. Hundreds of them lined up in perfect formation in front of the planes. They marched to orders called out by several of their leaders. All at once, as if they had been ordered to "run like hell," hundreds of soldiers dropped their bags and ran into the crowd. I was searching on tip-toes. My neck was stretched to its limit but I still couldn't see him because there were army fatigues, people, and flags everywhere, all around.

Then, finally, I was in his arms before I even laid eyes on his face. I was first, after nine long months of waiting for Connor to come home, I was the one he came to first. When I finally saw him, he was red with sunburn. His hair was sun-bleached white. The desert had been a rough place to spend the last nine months. He was bigger, stronger, and just seemed manlier. I couldn't speak so I kissed his sunburned cheeks and hugged him with all my might. He put me down and placed an eyebrow-raising kiss on my lips right in front of our families. "Wow. Welcome home, Connor," was all I could manage when it was over. I was blushing and embarrassed but no one really cared. He received love from the rest of his welcome home committee with one arm around me the entire time. He did, however, let go of me for a moment to embrace his mother. All he wanted to do was go home to the trailer. Connor Hawthorn, gorgeous American war veteran, wanted to go home to the trailer.

"Thank you all so much for coming," Connor said as we

headed toward the parking lot near the landing field. "I wish I could just go home right now but we have to debrief and check everything in. It's probably going to be a few hours yet before I can leave base."

"That's ok son, we'll be at Lucy's waiting for you," Trudi said. Connor kissed both our mothers on their cheeks and gave me a quick kiss, not quite comparable to the first one. He trotted off to collect the bags he had dropped in formation and then caught up with other soldiers all heading toward big army-green trucks that were taking them to debrief.

Endless hours passed. His family finally gave up and returned to their motel room. Mary returned to Judd Street. Dad went from sleeping in his chair to sleeping in his bed. Mom held out the longest but eventually decided to go to bed too. "He's probably not coming this late, Lucy. You may as well go on to bed."

"I know but I can't sleep; too much in my head right now."

"OK. Well, let me know if he calls or shows up."

"I will. Good night."

Sleep finally came over me like a slow descent into darkness. Restless, uneasy dreams shoved their way into my subconscious. Connor was lost in the desert just wondering around, sweating, with the sun beating down on him dressed in desert fatigues and combat boots. An assault rifle was slung over his shoulder. He turned around and his eyes met mine. Tears were streaming down his face cutting vertical streaks through the caked on sand. This unexpected eye-contact with Connor startled me awake. I had never seen him cry. I sat up on the couch. The digital clock on the kitchen counter read 1:45am. Disappointed as I could be, I put on my night shirt in the quiet darkness of my tiny room. Morrissey was the right soundtrack for me at this moment so I played the record on low and laid down on my tiny bed, alone. I had imagined a more eventful night, a hot and passionate welcome home, but it had only been filled, so far, with unanswered anticipation.

Not even a phone call. Where was Connor and what he was doing? Maybe he fell asleep in the barracks or maybe his commanding officers wouldn't let him leave for some reason. The hateful voice in my head began asking, "What if he went out with his buddies instead of coming here? What if he went to Nevo or to Judd Street? What if he decided he doesn't want you anymore?" The thoughts were too hard to bear and a little over dramatic. Of course, Connor wanted me. I was being ridiculous and insecure. I was being just who I've always been. "Poor Connor. You really picked a winner," I said sort of out loud. Morrissey seemed to agree with every self-loathing lyric.

Like a sixth sense or something I pulled back the blue and pink checkered curtain that hung over the window at the head of my bed to check for Connor one more time before burying my head in my pillow and crying myself to sleep. A red Jetta was parked along the edge of our corner lot. Connor was sitting in the driver's seat. He was out there alone. How long had he been there? Why didn't he let me know? Wait...Connor Hawthorn was sitting in his car in my front yard!!! I slipped on my flip flops, quietly unlocked the front door and raced to him. He reached over from his seat and opened the door for me.

"Hi." That was all I could manage. He looked at me with swollen, red eyes; cheeks wet with tears. The second time I had seen Connor cry tonight. "My God, baby. What's wrong?" I said reaching over to give him a hug.

"I went to the motel where my family is staying...they came

all this way, you know. I had to go see them before they leave in the morning. Mom told me...she told me about my grandfather. He's gone. I had to come here. I just want you to hold me right now."

"Let's go inside," I said. Mom and Dad never heard us come in, or slip down the hall to my room and close the door.

We sat side by side on my tiny bed, completely embraced, and I held him while he cried; his face buried in my neck. Connor had showered at the base and was dressed in jeans, a black t-shirt, and his favorite black high-tops. He smelled irresistible; clean like soap and cologne. I was in awe of his vulnerability and his willingness to open up to me like this. What I really wanted to do was kiss him and make love to him right then. Instead, I said, "I'm so sorry you had to come home to this news. I know how much you loved him." Nothing else was said. We lay down together, holding each other. He fell asleep. I kissed his soggy, burning hot cheek and soon dreamed of him again, the usual sweet and sensual kind.

CHAPTER 16

It did not take long for our old routines to fall back into place. He was there to pick me up from school or work. He was there to eat dinner, talk with my dad about being in the Middle East, flatter my mom with compliments about her cooking, and sometimes stay until 4am when he would grab his bag and quietly slip out of my reach.

My senior year was almost over and I had fulfilled all expectations. College acceptance letters came in but only one stayed on top of the stack: "You have been accepted to attend the University of North Carolina at Chapel Hill." I knew I wanted to go but there were complications beyond what my inexperienced mind could handle. Connor was almost finished with his four-year enlistment and had already told me that he couldn't wait to get back to Georgia. How would this work? Who would give-in? Would we compromise?

Friday night at the Record Exchange had been slow and easy. Arthur blasted Guns N' Roses for the last hour while we did our closing duties which involved straightening CDs and records in the stacks. Connor came in and sat on a stool beside the counter. "Lucy, go ahead, I got this," Arthur urged under his breath.

"No, Arthur, I'm not leaving you to close up by yourself," I whispered back.

"Look, I don't mean to be rude, but if I had someone here looking like that waiting for me, you'd be closing up alone."

"He is gorgeous isn't he?"

"Hell yeah, I'd date him and I'm not even like that." We both laughed as we glanced up at Connor who saw us and gave a little wave. I took him up on his offer, grabbed my purse from the back room, and walked up to my man.

"Hey Miss Bells, are you ready to go? You can leave now?"

"Yeah, let's go," I said stealing a kiss. Connor waved to Arthur on our way out of the door.

Instead of heading toward home, as usual, we took another route, a familiar yet neglected route. The road to Judd Street was filled with nostalgia. I had missed it; the music, the aura, the people. "Are you taking me to Judd Street, Connor?" He didn't answer; only looked over at me and tenderly touched my cheek with the backs of his fingers. He was in a quiet, serious mood just like in Washington during the hours before we first made love.

This must be serious. We sped down the hilly residential road while New Order's "Age of Consent" blasted from our open windows.

It was so quiet when Connor parked the car in the front yard. This was Friday night and the Judd Street house was strangely empty...no cars, no crowd, no music. We walked in the unlocked front door and Connor led me by the hand to Tory's room. He pressed play on the stereo-cassette player and Robert Smith quietly sang "Love Song" while Connor got down on one knee in front of me. He held my left hand cupped between his as he would sometimes do and said, "Remember when we had our first kiss right here in this room?" I nodded. "I asked Tory if I could have a little while with just us here tonight so she made sure everyone would be at Nevo."

"Ok," I whispered.

"I wanted to ask you something."

Again, I whispered, "Ok."

He pulled a ring from his pants pocket. It was a silver band with one little diamond perched right on top. "Lucy Bells, would you consider spending the rest of your life with me?"

****

So, this is the part where things go wrong. You are probably going to hate me for it but I have lived enduring the regret, so don't judge me too harshly. Isn't a girl allowed a moment of fear-spiked adrenaline? Isn't a girl allowed to run scared just a little before stepping into forever with the man of her dreams? Can't a girl make a mistake without paying for it for the rest of her life? This is the part where I begin to let go, backing into my quiet, solitary world; the world before Connor Hawthorn picked me out of the Judd Street crowd. But that world didn't exist anymore. Connor had changed me completely. Even still, like a fool, I thought if I kept us closed up in the tiny glass world I had created we would surely die. So I let him go, just like my fireflies. I let us go never imagining we could really end; foolishly believing he would still be there for me when my fear subsided. But I have always been wrong.

****

I was staring at the ring when my eyes blinked and rolled to meet his. Tears dropped from his emerald eyes. Seconds passed like pine sap while a sinister version of my life flashed before my eyes. In my demented imagination, I saw Connor's parents' house with us living in it, my pregnant belly, and a baby in a crib.

I saw Connor turn away from me, and then I was looking at myself with a bruised eye and a swollen lip.

That final image jerked me back to reality, to Tory's room where Connor was on his knee in front of me still holding the ring between his pointer and thumb. It is true, I didn't have many examples of positive relationships between a man and a woman placed before me, but Connor and I were different. I couldn't believe at this most special moment my masochistic mind had just predicted me as Connor's battered wife. Anyway, isn't the whole my-life-flashed-before-my-eyes thing supposed to happen before you almost die? This was just wrong. I shook my head in disbelief at what I had just seen and the word "no" carelessly tumbled out. "No, I don't mean to you...I mean...yes. I will." We both cried now. He slipped the ring on my finger and we hugged.

My mind should have been overcome with excitement from his proposal and ecstasy from this seduction. Instead, it was buzzing with confusion, fear, and guilt for having those horrible thoughts about Connor, none of which he deserved. I wanted to go home to my little room and listen to my records. I wanted to be alone. I couldn't believe it. I had him. He was mine. Connor Hawthorn was mine. Why couldn't I just let myself be happy? Why not just clear my head and be in the moment, right there, making love to Connor? "Are you ok, babe?" he finally asked. I guess he could tell something was wrong.

"Lucy, I can't wait for you to be my wife," he said as he stood up and put himself back together. I have always wondered if he noticed my distressed expression.

"Connor, can we wait to tell everyone? I mean, this is such a huge thing and..."

"Of course, we can. It's all up to you," he said holding out his hand to help me up off the floor. "It's all up to you," he said again hugging me and stroking my hair. Why did he have to leave it up to me? He took charge of everything else; why not this too? I was sure to ruin it.

We left Judd Street before the after-party began. The ride across town had been quiet except for Depeche Mode imploring us to "Enjoy the Silence." Connor drove while I alternately stared straight out the windshield or down at my left hand. I loved him; that was not a question in my mind, but I had fears that ranged from not being the perfect wife to actually being the perfect wife. Being married was something I never dreamed of before I met Connor. It was like I wanted more from my life but I wanted Connor too and for some reason, I felt like I had to choose. I was too conflicted to be happy. The ring stayed on my finger until we arrived at my parents' corner lot.

"I wish I could come in but I have to get back to base tonight. We have some shit going on tomorrow morning. God, sorry about my mouth. Being around soldiers all the time is not good for the manners."

I smiled and kissed his hand that had been squeezing my fingertips. "What should I tell my parents?"

"Don't tell them anything yet. We can do it together, later on. I know this is a lot to swallow right now."

"I love you, Connor," I said as I reached over and placed my right hand behind his head to pull him closer.

While we were kissing, Connor slipped the engagement ring off my finger and put it in the palm of my hand, "When the time is right."

"Thank you for understanding," I said getting out of his car. I closed the door and my beautiful soldier blew me a kiss before driving away.

I knew right then I was losing my mind. I wasn't going to let myself have the man beyond my dreams. Sabotage was the perfect solution for this little sadomasochist. Inexperience and fear flowed through my veins like a toxic cocktail. To say that I messed it up would be a huge understatement.

Thankfully, my parents were already asleep. I walked straight to my room and placed my token of Connor's undying love for me in my jewelry box. At least I thought his love was undying. I thought he loved me to the ends of the earth. But I have always been wrong.

CHAPTER 17

The heart is deceitful above all things, and desperately
wicked: who can know it?
- Jeremiah 17:9

onnor's ability to lead, his self-discipline, and his overall excellence did not go unnoticed by his offi-cers. They had plans for him that did not involve friv-olous things like time off to spend with his girlfriend, fiancée, or whatever they thought I was, if they even knew I existed.

"Hey Miss Bells," he said when I answered the phone.

"Hey Connor."

"I won't be able to call you by that name for very much longer. Did you tell anyone yet?"

"No. I'm waiting for you."

"Well, it's going to have to wait a while then. I'm going to an-other base somewhere out west. They're sending me to leader-ship school...it's an officer candidate thing for enlisted grunts."

"That's great, baby. I'm proud of you even though I want you to be here."

"Me too but I have to do this. I'll be back in three weeks. Then we can tell our parents and everyone else."

"When do you leave?"

"Tomorrow morning. It sucks, I know, but it's just like that. The army doesn't care about inconveniencing me. I'm on their watch for the next year and a half. It'll be ok. I'll make it up to you when I get back. Don't worry."

"Oh, I know you will. I'm already looking forward to it," I said with a hint of playful seduction in my voice.

"Don't make this harder than it already is, Miss Bells. Be good while I'm away."

"I will. I love you. Bye."

This was just the break my foolish heart thought it needed. Connor had been gone for a week with no phone call and I was surprisingly okay with that. Every time I walked into my tiny room, my eyes shamefully shifted to the jewelry box that contained our engagement ring. I refused to look at it because it scared me too much. I needed to be away from home, from that little ring that caused me so much confusion, and so I found my way back over to Judd Street.

Tory and I worked together that first Friday night he was gone. Mary arrived to pick us up around closing time.

"So why did Connor need our house all to himself the other night?" Tory inquired with a smirk and a wink toward Mary as if she already knew too much.

"Well, Lucy, what did you and Connor do with all your private time?" Mary said teaming up with her best friend.

"I don't know what you're talking about. We went there but it was only because he wanted time alone with me to talk. That's all," I said.

"Okay. But you really need to practice lying more often because you suck at it."

"I'll take that as a compliment, Tory. Anyway, what do you think I'm lying about?"

"Let's just say you two were not the only ones in the house," Tory said.

"And that person wasn't at all happy about it either," Mary added.

"Someone was there?" My face must have turned scarlet with embarrassment as I remembered…"Who was it?" I was pissed.

"It doesn't matter," Tory said. "You won't tell us anything so we won't tell you. But really, it's not that hard to guess, Lucy."

It dawned on me…Pan.

Mary drove us to Judd Street. I wanted to see Pan to ask him why he had spied on us; why he had told our business. But Pan was nowhere to be seen. Andrew still treated me like an honored guest only this time he wanted to know every detail about Connor.

"Is he good in bed? I know he is, girl. He is so gorgeous. Do you know how lucky you are, Lucy?" I just smiled and looked at the floor. "Even still, you better be careful. I don't trust these army guys. You're too good for any of them. You better let me know if he does anything stupid."

"I will, Andrew. You'll be the first to know." I guess he never suspected I was going to be the one to do something stupid.

I sat in my old corner chair while the after-party crowd came trickling in. I could feel myself slipping further and further away from Connor. I was purposefully trying to let him go while searching for a way out. I didn't want to get married, not even to Connor, and I had my reasons.

I knew that marriage changed people. My mom taught me that lesson when I was just a little girl. Late one evening in a violent fit of rage, my dad had thrown the old iron typewriter he used to type out his sermons across the room at my mom. It crashed through the wall leaving a big gaping hole in the sheet rock. She rushed Mary and me into the car and drove us to Dairy Queen, her idea of compensation for having to witness such violence. She told us a story about when she and Dad got married.

"My mama and her sisters put so much effort into my wedding," she said with a smile. It still excited her to think back on it after almost twenty years. "Aunt Ellie made all the bridesmaids and junior bridesmaids' dresses and that was a lot of sewing because there were twenty of them all together. She also made my wedding dress. I remember teams of little old church ladies coming to sit at our house for hours to hand stitch sequins and embroidery on that dress. It was quite an event."

"There was a lot of cooking and decorating. Our wedding cake was like something out of a magazine, all homemade. A lot goes into planning a wedding." Mary and I sat silent and still while she remembered out loud all that remained of her own love story.

"And Bobby had been so excited with every detail, you know, making sure his tux fit and that the suits were ready for his father and groomsmen. He was a perfect gentleman, believe it or not, but my parents still didn't like him. They didn't think he was good enough for me since he grew up in an old slave shack set back in the woods on the outskirts of town with no plumb-ing or running water. His father was an alcoholic and he and his brothers would sometimes have to fight him off their mother. And she was mean as hell, too. Your dad wanted a better life, but I guess some things are just in your blood."

Mary, only ten years old at the time, was on the front seat star-ing out of the side window. I was in the back seat, only seven, and still shaken-up from watching my dad throw a typewriter at my mom that missed her head by an inch. "Bobby really tried. He really did. He drove the school bus and did other odd jobs to make some money. He even bought an old car, a '53 Chevy, and fixed it up, he and your Uncle Fink. I admired him for that and I loved him. But after all that planning and cooking and sewing, after we stood in front of a church filled with every-one we knew and said, "I do," we got into his car all decorated with strings and cans, and he broke my heart for the first time."

Mary finally looked over at her and said, "What did he do?"

"Well, I got in the front seat and he was in the driver's seat, of course. I slipped over to the middle seat and hooked my arm into his and I even remember laying my head on his shoul-der. When we drove away from the church, he took his arm and pushed me off as hard as he could. He said, 'Stay over there. You don't have to do all that now. We're married. Act like it.' I'll never forget his words or how it felt to be shoved off his arm. I couldn't believe it. And from that moment, he was just different. I don't know why he changed but it was certainly a disappointment. I never told anybody that story. I just wanted you to know that I didn't marry a monster. He was a good man before he just changed, all of a sudden."

I learned early-on from my mom in the back seat of the car on the way to Dairy Queen that people could not be trusted.

****

Too much fear. Too much unknown. Too much of everything too fast. I needed to get back to my old familiar solitude. And so I sat in my corner chair and watched Judd Street in action that Friday night while trying to channel the old Lucy; the one who was going to college, the one who was a loner; the one who avoided attention. The crowd became intolerable and Andrew had apparently forgotten that I didn't need to be around all the smoke and beer. He was in the kitchen entertaining his guests and not worrying about me. I had to get out. I took the staircase thinking I was just going to hide out in Mary's room but instead, Pan's closed door caught my attention.

I lightly knocked. When no one answered, I turned the doorknob and slowly opened the door. Everyone, including me, thought Pan had gone off on one of his frequent escapes. He was mysterious like that and would sometimes just disappear for days at the time. It was dark and heavy with the scent of incense. Slowly and quietly I crept into his room and gently closed the door behind me. I just wanted to be near him. I wasn't mad at him anymore. Actually, I missed him and wanted to talk to him about my feelings and doubts about getting married. I thought he would understand my desire to avoid the attention it would bring. A whisper came from the pitch dark corner, "Lucy. Come here." It was Pan.

I followed the sound of his voice across the creaking hardwood floor. He reached up and took my hand when I got close enough. I had never touched Pan before. I always imagined his skin would be cold and hard like a vampire but it wasn't. His hands were soft and clammy. He pulled me down to my knees and then to my surprise, he leaned in and kissed my neck. I felt a strange rush and pushed back. He pulled me closer and placed his lips on mine. I mindlessly kissed him back. "Pan, wait. What are we doing?" I whispered as he reached his long fingers up the back of my shirt and unhooked my bra. Of course he didn't answer. His body pushed mine to the floor; he was on top of me and I didn't resist. In contrast to his passion, I must have felt like a corpse beneath him. It wasn't love like it was with Connor. How could I be doing this to us? I wanted to rewind, go back to the top of the stairs and just stay the course to Mary's room. We both sighed once more and it was done.

Yes, it certainly was done. Connor was no longer my only one. "I'm sorry, Lucy." Pan whispered into my ear while kissing my neck. "I know you're engaged to that asshole but it's wrong. I'm the one who has loved you for so long now and I know you love me."

Not allowing what he said to sink in, I whispered, "Oh my God. What the fuck just happened?"

He pulled the black hair away from his blue, glistening eyes barely exposing his beautiful pale face in the darkness. He kissed my closed lips once more and laid his head on my chest while our breathing slowed to normal. I wanted to get up and just run from that house. I wanted to run away from what I had just done. I let Connor go for just a moment and now everything had changed.

While I was lying there not really knowing what to do in those awkward seconds that seemed to stretch on for hours, the door swung open and light flooded the room like a big accusing finger pointing right at my guilty bare breasts. None of Pan's roommates would have invaded his room like that. It was a soldier and a girl looking for some privacy. It was one of Connor's friends, the one with the red pickup. "Holy shit is that..." Yep, he saw me.

"Turn out the fucking light!" Pan yelled interrupting Connor's friend. I had never heard his voice above a whisper. He quickly stood, pulling up his pants, and slammed the door with them on the other side. I could hear the girl laughing, drunk, as they stumbled back down the steps. I knew Connor's friend had recognized me.

"This will not end well." That was all I could say as I pulled down my shirt and walked toward the door, toward Pan. There was a vulnerable tenderness and sincerity about him that just killed me but I was dying inside from something else: regret. I brushed past his open arms, left his room, and closed Mary's door behind me. I peeped out of her window and felt relieved to see the red pickup pulling out of the yard.

I fell on her bed and cried into a pillow. Connor was the only one who could ever have my heart and my passion; only Connor, and now I was sure. No one else could love me like he did. No one else could make my heart beat faster with a glance or give me chill bumps with a simple touch. No one else affected me like Connor. He alone completed me and now it was too late. I would soon know what devastating rejection feels like on the other side of the Herrmann-Hawthorn "no regrets, no look-backs." One fear and confusion-induced time of infidelity just to be sure that I was sure and that was all it took. One mistake was all it took.

Life used to be so simple in my corner chair before I entered Pan's room. Now I was a scheming, frantic, soon-to-be liar, or soon-to-be self-incriminator. I was leaning toward liar. I couldn't imagine telling Connor what had just happened and with whom. Would he cry? Would he try to physically hurt Pan (what an unfair fight that would be)? Maybe he would understand if I explained how I was feeling before this happened. I was confused and freaking out. But the result of my terrible indiscretion was that I figured it out; I knew I could marry Connor now. I couldn't stand the thought of another man touching me or kissing me. I was ready to compromise. These were all pitiful attempts at finding a bright side to what I had done to Connor and me. I was ready to do whatever it took to keep him, so I opted for liar. In fact, I just wouldn't mention it; not to Connor, Mary, or anyone. And I prayed that Connor's friend with the red pickup was too drunk to remember what he had seen, although I imagine witnessing his friend's bare-breasted girlfriend underneath another boy is a pretty unforgettable sight.

Minutes passed. "Hey Lucy. Did you see Pan up here earlier? He just left with his duffle bag. No one even knew he was here," Mary said sounding concerned about her housemate.

"No," I lied. "But can you take me home?"

"Sure. Are you ok?"

"Yeah," I lied with a ridiculous inflection in my voice. "I just need to go home." (Maybe this lying thing will be easier than I thought.)

On the ride across town, Mary and Tory sat in the front and blasted The Cure while I sat in the back and prayed: "Dear God,

92

Please forgive me for what I have done. You know my heart better than I do. You know I love Connor. Please give me direction and help me to know what to do."

Like a father hell-bent on accountability and discipline, I actually heard in my mind the following omnipotent reprimand: "You should have prayed this prayer before you opened Pan's door. You will have to work this one out on your own." I felt an overwhelming sense of dread.

CHAPTER 18

It was Sunday, a week after I had taken that fateful detour into Pan's room and set my life on an unexpected course. For days I had thought about how my first efforts to socialize with the human race had turned out to be disastrous. I now harbored secrets. Not just innocent ones but huge ones like becoming engaged to Connor and cheating on him within the same week. Amid of all this heightened emotion, I had to complete my senior project which was a forty-page essay on the evolution of public schools in America since the 1800s. It's no surprise that my mind could hardly focus on this assignment while sitting on my bed; the same bed where Connor and I had spent many nights confessing and showing our love for one another. I had to get out of that room; the same room that sheltered my engagement ring to Connor. So I called Judd Street. Thankfully Mary answered. "Hey, would you mind coming to get me? I need to finish my paper, but I can't concentrate here," I told her.

"Yeah, I'll come. Just give me an hour." I gathered my things and waited for her on the front steps.

"Have you heard from Connor?" Mary asked me on the way to Judd Street.

"No, not yet," I said fearing any more discussion on this topic.

"How much longer is he going to be away," she continued.

"I guess he has like two more weeks or so. I really need to get my mind focused on this paper. It's due before graduation," I said trying to change the subject.

"When is graduation; soon, right? I hope Connor will be home," she persisted.

"Yeah, it's a couple of days after he gets home. I haven't spoken to him so I'm not sure if his plans have changed." And the conversation just kept getting worse.

"So Pan has been gone all week and nobody knows where he is."

"Well, that's not really so strange, is it? I mean, he's kind of like that anyway, right?" I said.

"Yeah, but Andrew is worried for some reason. I think something might have happened and he's just not telling us." I stared straight out the front window. If Mary had seen my expression, she would have known something was terribly wrong. What did Andrew know about Pan? Had Pan confided in him? What would Andrew think of me if he knew what I had done to Pan and to Connor? I felt like the lowest element that existed on earth. Way worse than the "trailer park trash" I had feared becoming for all those years.

We finally arrived at Judd Street. This was Sunday afternoon so of course no one was there except the housemates, minus one. I took a seat at the dining room table and spread out my notes and started to work on my paper. The house was silent and still for about an hour until Andrew, Mary, Tory, and Evan gathered in the living room. Not even paying my presence any attention, they began a house meeting. I knew they did this once a month to settle bills and discuss issues but this one was different. Andrew began, "I spoke to Pan's father this morning. Apparently, Pan went home and overdosed on some of his mother's migrain medication. His father told me that a lot had happened in the past year before he moved in with us. He told me his best friend had been killed in a car accident and that Pan was driving the car but walked away without a scratch. They had been drinking and smoking pot. He dropped out of school after that. There was a lot of drama going on at home. That's why he was at Nevo so much before we offered him his room. His parents paid the rent because they thought maybe it was the best thing for him. Anyway, he was in the hospital for two days but he's been discharged and they don't know where he is right now." Evan whispered, "Oh my God." Mary and Tory looked sad and worried. Andrew continued, "If he comes here, we have to be careful not to push him too far...I mean we can't let him know that we know. Just try to act normal." Everyone agreed.

I sat in the dining room feeling accused and guilty. Did I cause this to happen? Was this even about me at all? This was certainly not the right place to come work on my paper. I wondered if I should ask Mary to take me back home or call my mom to come get me. I didn't want to be here if Pan showed up. That might cause him more anguish.

The conversation in the living room came to a close and everyone dispersed, except Andrew. He came into the dining room and sat across from me. In his best efforts to show concern for what I was doing, he said, "What are you working on?"

"It's my senior project...an essay about education," I said just trying to appease him without getting too in-depth.

"Well, can you take a couple of minutes to talk to me about

something? It won't take long and then I'll leave you alone. I'm just curious about something." "Yeah, sure," I said tossing my pen down thinking this was going to be the confrontation I wanted to avoid.

"Did you hear what we were discussing in there? Did you hear what I said about Pan?"

"Well, yeah. I mean I overheard that he's missing," I said only offering half the truth.

"Well, Lucy, there's more to it than that. I had to go into his room and search around a little bit, just looking for some sign as to where he might be. I found his journal under his mattress and I read some of it...the last few pages just trying to figure out what has happened to him in the last few days and where he might be right now." Andrew put his elbows on the table, covered his face with both hands, and sighed. I sat perfectly still and silent bracing for the bomb to drop. "Did you know that all this time Pan has secretly been in love with you?" Andrew said behind his hands.

"No, that's absurd," I lied.

"Well, unless his journal is filled with lies, it's not really so absurd. He wrote about you in detail. He wrote about you and Connor having sex in Tory's room. He saw the whole thing...the proposal that no one else knows about. I would never tell anyone else but I'm just letting you know what I read. Is that part true...about you and Connor?"

"Yes," and that was all I could offer in response.

"Well, it might have pushed him over the edge. His journal is filled with his thoughts about you. He wrote down things you said, outfits you have worn, he wrote about watching you and Connor sitting and talking together. He really has deep feelings

97

for you, Lucy."

I guess Pan didn't write about how I had entered his dark room and followed the sound of his voice. I guess he didn't describe how I knelt in front of him and selfishly misled him to believe that I wanted him. I wonder how Andrew would have treated me if he knew how I gave myself to Pan and didn't stop it from happening or how I carelessly brushed past him and closed Mary's door just minutes after having sex with him. What would he think of me if he knew how I had used Pan in a vain attempt to let Connor go?

"Andrew, I don't know what to say. I just hope he's ok." He came around the table and hugged me, still believing in my innocence and goodness, even though both virtues had taken a beating in the last few days. For now, it seemed that Pan and I were the only two who knew about our indiscretion. I was forgetting one extremely important fact: Connor's friend with the red pickup had seen me on my back with Pan on top of me, but I would soon remember.

I sat at the table for another hour or so working on my paper between lapses of composure, prayer, and silent fits of panic while my spot on the earth slowly turned away from the sun. Chinese food was ordered and delivered. "Come on over here, Lucy. I got you some sweet and sour chicken with veggie rice, your favorite," Mary said. I gathered my papers into a neat pile on the table and headed into the living room where all the housemates, minus one, were sitting, talking, and eating together. We sat around the coffee table piled with food containers, bottles of beer, cans of Mountain Dew, and lit candles competing for space. The conversation was light and upbeat which was a needed break considering the heavy topic on everyone's mind. Tory's infectious laughter even made an appearance once or twice.

I was not prepared for what soon happened. The front door opened and Pan stepped into the house. He was clutching the duffle bag hanging from his shoulder. His hair was pulled back under a baseball cap and he was wearing blue jeans and a t-shirt. He looked so different, like a normal, beautiful boy. His eyes were still glistening blue but instead of worried, they seemed to be smiling tonight. Tory and Mary jumped up and hugged him at the same time.

"I'm so glad you're home," Tory said.

"Don't leave us like that again. No more of that, ok?" Mary said.

"Okay, okay. Easy does it," Pan said with a smile. He came over to the table, picked up an egg roll and ate it in two bites. "God, that's good. How is everybody?" he asked while looking straight at me. I didn't answer him. Evan and Andrew filled in the empty space with replies but I couldn't speak. I also couldn't take my eyes off of him. He had just tried to kill himself and now he seemed more relaxed and happy than I had ever seen him.

He stepped around Andrew and Mary to where I was sitting on the couch. He put his hand on my shoulder and kissed the top of my head. Andrew looked on with confused disapproval. Then Pan said, "I'm really tired...going to bed, guys. Andrew, we'll talk in the morning, ok."

"Are you sure, Pan? I can come up now, I mean, we can talk now if you're up for it. I don't mind," Andrew urged.

"Nope. Tomorrow," Pan said heading for the stairs. He looked back at us sitting there and caught my eye. He said, "Goodbye" and headed up to his room. There was a part of me that wanted to run behind him, go back into his room, and hold him all night; only this time I would be a caring friend instead of a lying cheat. But it was too late for that. The conversation turned to whispers about Pan, not gossip, just genuine concern and relief that he was back and safe upstairs in his room.

On the way to take me home, Mary and Tory opted to talk instead of blast music.

"We are going to have to get Pan out more. He needs a life," Mary began.

"Yeah, but he's so shy. When he's at Nevo, he just sits alone or dances alone…he's always alone," Tory responded.

"Well, we can just be there more, you know, knock on his door a little more and just be around him more," Mary suggested.

"I don't know, Mary. He seems most comfortable with Andrew, like he's the big brother he never had. I don't know how I would have dealt with the whole car accident thing. I don't think we should ever let him know that we know."

"I agree," Mary said. "Pan just needs somebody to love. I wish he could meet someone special but I can't think of anyone good enough for him; you know someone who wouldn't shit on him and leave his broken heart more broken."

This was getting crazy. I was the girl who had already done exactly that, not only to Pan, but to Connor as well.

The road soon ended at the corner lot. We said our goodbyes and they pulled away. I looked back at the trailer and had never felt more at home.

While I lay in my bed commiserating with Morrissey, I was grateful that I still had over a week before Connor came back from his leadership training. I had to decide if I would tell him the truth or just conveniently not mention it. In Connor's absence, I had tested the dark waters of infidelity and had come away more certain than ever that I belonged with him, only him. In spite of this clarity, however, I didn't know how we could ever be the same. I was unsure how to handle it and I was without a soul in the world to counsel me: not my mom, not my sister or anyone on Judd Street considering how I had hurt Pan, and of course not Connor. Even God had shaken his head and left me to squander in my filth alone. I was lulled into a restless sleep while Morrissey sang a foreshadowing lyric, "There is a light that never goes out. There is a light that never goes out. There is a light that never goes out. There is a light…"

CHAPTER 19

Some days are unmemorable. You know you woke up and had breakfast, showered, went to school, work, or whatever, but nothing happens to mark its existence except that you lived through it and are now older because of it. This day is one I remember well although I shouldn't. It should have just been a random Monday morning that I went to school to finish my senior essay. I should have just received my invitations for graduation (one for Mom, Mary, and Connor since Dad was too feeble to attend) and then practiced playing Pomp and Circumstance with the orchestra until it was ringing in my head. I shouldn't remember this particular time that Mom drove me to my four-hour night shift at The Record Exchange, but this day was one that I will never forget. From the moment the sun rose, it shone its light on a terrible tragedy. I didn't know until I got to work just how wrong this day had been.

"Isn't Tory supposed to work tonight?" I asked Arthur who was sitting behind the counter.

"Yep, but something ain't right on Judd Street. She won't be in tonight," he replied.

"What happened?"

"Well, I don't know the full story but I think somebody died... one of the roommates." How could he offer that information so nonchalantly?

"Arthur...what? Who...what are you saying? Was somebody killed?" I knew it couldn't have been Mary because Mom would have known. I knew it wasn't Tory because Arthur would have known. That leaves Andrew, Evan, and... "Oh my God, Pan?"

"Yeah, that's it. He's the one," Arthur confirmed.

"Pan is dead? Oh my God. How?"

"Lucy, you should just call Mary. Go to the back room and call her 'cause I don't really know that much about it," Arthur said. He was right. I had to call Mary.

"Hello?" Mary said with a shaky voice. "Mary, what happened? What is going on?"

"Pan is dead. Andrew found him this morning. He hung himself." She was unable to say anything more.

"Hello?" Andrew said taking the phone from her.

"Hey, I'm at work. I just found out."

"Don't worry Lucy. This is not because of you. Pan had a lot of issues. We are all devastated but I can't talk right now. His father is here. Gotta go now, sweetie," and hung up the phone.

Andrew had said, "This is not because of you," but he didn't know the whole story, did he?

Arthur's friends had shown up since this was supposed to be his night off. He mostly hung out with them in the back room. I sat behind the counter on this painfully slow random Monday night thinking about Pan. I imagined Pan's lifeless body lying on a metal table in a morgue. I imagined his blue eyes behind his closed lids and his black hair against his white skin. I imagined the dark bruise across his broken neck. Death was just weird and I had no experience dealing with it. I felt deep sadness for Pan but mostly just a sense of strange finality. I would never see

Pan again and that was just...weird.

Mary and Andrew came to pick me up after work. Andrew wanted to be there to talk to me and answer my questions if I had any. He was such a caretaker. I know he took on Pan's suicide as a personal failure for not being there to stop him; for not seeing his intent.

On the way across town to take me home, he openly talked about what he had seen during the early morning hours on this random Monday. "I woke up around eight o'clock and knew that Pan and I were going to have a talk about his best friend who had died. I was going to tell him that I had been in his journal, not snooping but just trying to figure out where he was for those two days he was missing. And I was going to talk to him about you, Lucy, and how much you and Connor are in love and that maybe he should try to find someone else to go out with, you know just have some fun. Well, I went to the kitchen first to fix my coffee like I always do and I ate a piece of toast with butter on it while I waited for it to brew." Andrew was beginning to fall apart now, his voice was cracking and tears were welling. "All this time, Pan was hanging by his neck...dead...with the full light of the sun shining on him while I wasted time messing around in the fucking kitchen." Andrew cleared his throat and gained composure. "I poured two cups of coffee, one for me and one for him, and made my way back upstairs. I remember thinking how strange that I could actually see the sun's light shining around the door frame, you know, because he never had his shade pulled up and it was always dark in his room. And then I just opened the door and there he was. God, it was so awful. I dropped both cups of coffee and ran over to him. He was so heavy and I couldn't get him down at first. I had to stand on the crate he had kicked over and untie his father's necktie and then we both fell to the floor." Mary pulled around the cul-de-sac to our corner lot and parked the car. Andrew pulled a piece of paper from his pocket. Through tears and with shaking voice and hands, he read the poem that Pan had written and taped to his exposed window:

I fear I walk in shadows breath
Holding hands with something gone
I'm left here in this mellow room
Where the candles burn out too fast.
Fearing sleep for new days come
And this same room and this same air
Will greet me in the morning's glare
And hold me stiff like death and boards
Together clasped around my bed
And when the sun's pale red shadows pass along the walls
Slowly getting close to me
I'll let the shadows fall.

The sun rose this morning at five-thirty. Pan was hanging there in the glaring light while I got ready for school, ate my bowl of cereal, rode to school with Mom, wrote my essay, and received my graduation invitations. Andrew was passing through the gates of hell while I was playing Pomp and Circumstance over and over with the orchestra. This is how I remember that random Monday that I should not remember; everything I did was on a timeline labeled, "Pan's Suicide."

I reached up and hugged Andrew and Mary.

"Do you want to come in, I mean, I know it's going to be hard to be at Judd Street now," I said.

"No Sweetie, I have to get back. I love you," Andrew said.

"I love you too...both of you," I replied.

It was around 11:00pm when I walked in the trailer. Mom and Dad were already in bed, and a note was taped to the bar. It said, "LUCY!! Connor called. He'll be home tomorrow night. He can't wait to see you. Love, Mom." That was my last straw, my breaking point, my end-of-the-road. I took the note, walked to my little room, fell on my little bed, and cried into my pillow until sleep finally rescued me.

That night was the first time I dreamed of Simon Pantell, who called himself "Pan." I was not there that dreadful morning to witness it, but my morbid dreams have played it over and over: Pan suspended in the air surrounded by the warm, glowing light of the sun; the same glaring light he had avoided for so many years. He was eighteen and beautiful, lost in a world where he did not fit. Sadness and disappointment had mercilessly cloaked him, but now he was free to fly away.

CHAPTER 20

C onnor was coming home on Tuesday night. I was graduating from high school on Friday morning. I tried to take my mom's advice and focus on the good things happening in my life. It was just so damn hard for me to do. I was hoping that I could pull it off; that I could keep calm and stable in front of Connor. I already knew what a terrible liar I was but I wasn't sure how developed my skills at deception and secrecy were. I was about to find out.

The phone rang around ten-thirty on Tuesday night. Mom and Dad had already gone to bed so I quickly picked up the receiver.

"Hello," I whispered, knowing it had to be Connor.

"Lucy, I'm coming to get you. I'll be there in twenty minutes."

He hung up the phone before I could answer. What did he mean by "I'm coming to get you?" Did he intend to take me somewhere? I became worried because of his curt and matter-of-fact manner of speaking. I was thinking he would have been more excited to hear my voice which led me to wonder if he, somehow, already knew my secret.

When Connor's red Jetta pulled around the cul-de-sac to the corner lot, I was already on the front steps, waiting. He didn't get out or cut the car off so I walked over and opened the passenger door not really knowing what to expect.

"Hey baby get in," Connor said. He grabbed the back of my head and pulled me over for a kiss that indicated to me he did not already know my secret. "I've rented us a room because I don't have the self-control I need to sneak around tonight. I am so happy to see you right now."

Connor continued to kiss me until I finally pulled away to say, "Well, what are you waiting for? Let's go."

Connor drove his car, not saying a word, while "Bizarre Love Triangle" blasted into the night from our open windows. (Seriously, this song right now?) He finally slowed down on the outskirts of town as we approached a seedy little dive called, The Queen Ann Motel. It was painted pink. One other car was parked out front. I looked at Connor with some obvious discontent. Did he really expect me to spend the night in this rat trap?

"Yes, this is it," Connor said, laughing at my expression. "We'll have fun if we just ignore the critters crawling around us. Can we do this, or do you object too much?" God, why couldn't I tell him no?

He already had the key so we headed to the door that had a number four plaque with a golden crown painted over it. He unlocked it.

"You go first and make sure there are no bugs or anything," I said.

Connor laughed and said, "You wish."

He picked me up like a bride, carried me into the room, tossed me onto the bed, and closed the door.

This episode took our relationship, our love life, to another level. How could I have even thought about letting this man go? After this night with Connor, I hardly considered what Pan and

I had done as sex. My conscience seemed to be clearing up just fine.

I finally said, "Welcome home, Connor. I missed you."

We both laughed out loud and I held onto him for dear life, thinking there was no way we could ever end.

We both hesitantly peeked around the dingy shower curtain and saw the grimy tub. Connor decided for us both, "Um, let's get the hell out of here." He left the room key right on the dresser and we headed for the car. On the way out of the gravel parking lot, Connor confessed, "Lucy, you just fulfilled one of my fantasies and this motel seemed like the perfect place. I just hope I didn't offend you or hurt you."

"You didn't, baby," I said stroking his scarlet cheek.

"It's our little secret then, okay?"

Looking at his perfect profile, I replied, "Okay, our little secret."

Fortunately, this was the kind of secret I didn't mind keeping because I shared it with Connor. We headed for the trailer while New Order's "Regret" blasted from our open windows. (These damn songs.)

I headed for the bathroom and Connor fell on the couch. When I came back up the narrow hallway, I could see him. He was already fast asleep. I went into my room, closed the door, and lay in my bed - mind spinning out of control. Then she started; my inner saboteur began to harass, "You probably caused Pan's tragic end and you act like you don't even care. How will you feel telling everyone that you and Connor are getting married when you have already cheated on him? Are you just giving up your dream to go to UNC? How does it feel to give up all control over your life?" I could feel myself slipping back into that deep, dark, doubtful corner so I actually said, just above a whisper, "Shut up, you jealous bitch," and turned over counting one...two while breathing in through my nose and three...four...five while breathing out through my mouth, over and over until I heard my door quietly open and close. I prayed a quick and silent, "Thank You," and welcomed Connor into my bed...into my arms with a tight, desperate embrace.

CHAPTER 21

****

"Three may keep a secret
if two of them are dead."
                                    - Benjamin Franklin

F riday morning came quickly. My high school graduation ceremony went as planned. Connor was there
with Mom and Mary. Everything was perfect for this
moment in time. It was the calm before the storm.

I always knew that socializing was not something I was meant
to do but the Judd Street housemates wanted to throw a little
graduation party for me. There was a nervous, sickening feeling in my stomach about going back to that house. It held my
secret and it held Pan's death. In spite of my dread, Connor
and I showed up to my party around eight o'clock that night.
The housemates, Connor, and I were the only ones there and it
would be hours before the after-party crowd arrived. The mood
was somber considering recent events, but everyone was trying to be upbeat. Andrew had even bought me a cake that read,
"Congratulations Lucy!" While we were standing around in the

kitchen eating, Andrew kept eyeing me and smiling. I figured it was because he knew about my engagement to Connor but no one else did. Mary finally presented what she believed to be a great idea: "Connor, you and Lucy should come to Nevo tonight. PLEEEASE. We'll have fun. Please come with us," she begged.

Evan added dryly, "It's better than staying here by your-selves."

Connor looked at me to gauge my reaction. I bought Evan's comment wholeheartedly considering my recent indiscretion with Pan and then his suicide. "Yeah, Connor, let's go dance among the Goths," I said shaking my head in submission.

"Are you serious, Lucy?"

"Sure. Why not? It'll be fun."

"Okay, but I'm driving my own car just in case I can't take it for very long." Then Connor put a piece of cake in my mouth and kissed me on the lips just like a groom would do to his bride at their reception. Andrew gasped and teared-up while placing his hand over his heart. I smiled at him and rolled my eyes a little, shaking my head at his dramatics.

While everyone prepared themselves for a Friday night at Nevo, Connor and I sat in the living room mostly making out in my corner chair. We certainly couldn't talk because the music filled every space in the house. Tonight it was Tory's choice, Jane's Addiction. As far as I was concerned, this was perfect; no talking, straddling Connor's lap while he kissed me softly on my lips, behind my ears, down my neck to my collar bones... holding me firmly with his hands, then his arms. This was my first taste of life beyond high school, but what had started so sweetly, was about to turn sour.

We walked into Nevo together. I tried to act like I wasn't nervous, but I was. Something about this place freaked me out a little, I mean, it was overwhelming. The music was so loud and the smoke that created the foggy atmosphere had a strange, strong smell. Connor and I found two stools at the bar and sat down. Andrew and Evan stood around us for a few minutes, sort of like babysitters, before they couldn't resist the pull of the music any longer. Connor and I sat there watching as the dance floor became crowded with Goths in chains, leather, lace, and boots. Connor was holding my hand and squeezing my fingertips to the beat of the music.

I am still filled with sadness even all these years later when I think back on those minutes that Connor and I sat beside each other on those barstools at Club Nevo. Those were the last minutes of Connor and Lucy. Those were the last minutes that Connor still believed I was his soul mate and still wanted me in his life. I had been careless with my secret. In fact, it wasn't really a secret at all. Connor's friend with the red pickup knew full-well what I had done with Pan in his dark room that night. Had I been more aware when we pulled into the Nevo parking lot, I might have seen the little red truck and insist we go home. But I wasn't thinking about that. I have learned that secrets and lies take time and effort. They must be nurtured and tended to. I was too inexperienced to know this then.

Out of the dense smoke, Connor's friend with the red pickup and his drunken girlfriend spilled onto the bar beside us. I was frozen with fear that he would recognize me. Of course, he would. How could he have forgotten? He had seen my naked breasts and bare legs; a boy on top of me and his bare ass. Of course, he would recognize me. Of course, he would. And so this is how my brief, yet permanent, love affair with Connor Hawthorn ended on that fateful high school graduation night at Club Nevo.

"Dude, what the fuck is up, man? I haven't seen you in forever, dude," Connor's drunk friend began.

They shook hands while Connor replied, "Yeah, how are you, man?" Then he looked over at me and shook his head, "He's really drunk right now but he is actually this obnoxious all the time," and winked. Did he notice how I was trying to hide my face, how I was turning my back to him and his friend? I should have walked away but I didn't. I sat there like I was just waiting for the tables to turn; like I was just waiting to take my punishment all at once right there in public.

"So where the fuck have you been, man?" Connor's friend continued, apparently unable to construct a sentence without the work "fuck."

"I've been away at training. Anyway, have you met my fiancée, Lucy Bells?" Connor proudly and innocently said, trying not to exclude me from his conversation. "Lucy, this is Darren, he used to be in my recon unit." I hesitantly and reluctantly turned toward Connor and his friend trying my best to just smile, shake his hand or whatever was expected, and then turn back away.

I guess these recon soldiers had an innate knack for remembering detailed observations. When I faced Darren and offeredmy hand to shake his, his expression changed from that of a deliriously happy, drunken man, to that of an angry soldier about to save his friend from an enemy. Connor noticed the change in mood and looked from Darren to me. I looked at Connor who was aware, just that quickly, that something was wrong. He looked down to see my hand was the only one extended. "Are you fucking serious, man? You bitch!" Darren reached out but only to slap my hand away. Connor immediately reacted by standing up between us. He put one hand on Darren's chest to push him away and said, "Are you crazy, man? What the fuck is wrong with you? Don't put your hands on her." Darren did not hesitate, "She fucked that dead dude, man. I saw it. I fucking saw it. Two weeks ago on Judd Street. I saw her fucking tits and everything man...she fucked that dude, Pan, or whatever the fuck his name was."

Connor glanced back and saw my face. It must have been pretty bad. Connor turned around, reached back and punched Darren right in the nose. Darren fell back and hit the floor...hard. His drunk girlfriend screamed and dropped to her knees beside him. The crowd turned toward us. Connor grabbed my wrist and forced our way through the crowd. He still held my wrist, too tightly, all the way to the car. I had to run a little just to keep up.

We pulled out of the parking lot and rode in silence for eternity until Connor finally said, "What was he talking about Lucy? Just tell me the truth now because you know I will find out." He looked at me with such desperation for this not to be happening and hit the steering wheel with his fist one time. He wanted this to be a lie, but I could tell that he knew it wasn't. So I told Connor the truth. I could not lie to him after all.

"I don't know what to say," I began.

"THE FUCKING TRUTH!" Connor yelled at me for the first and only time. I burst out crying, unable to handle what was happening. "Lucy, just tell me what happened. I'm sorry I yelled. Just tell me now, please. Let's just get this part over with, okay," Connor reassured.

"I...didn't...mean...to...I...was...just..." My words were coming out one at a time between little gasps as I tried to control my breathing.

"Calm down. It's ok." Connor reached over and stroked the back of my head. I took two deep breaths and summarized as best I could.

"I was scared to get married...and I went into Pan's room to talk...and it happened. (Gasp) I'm so sorry, Connor. (Gasp) God, I'm so sorry." I buried my face in my hands and cried.

Conner did not say another word. He chose to blast New Order's "Ruined in a Day" to drown out my crying. He pulled up to the corner lot and said, "Get the fuck out of my car."

Now the desperation of losing Connor took over. I begged and pleaded with him to understand why I had freaked out that night, to forgive me, and to give me another chance. I reached over to kiss him but his hands grabbed my arms and pushed me back to my seat. "I said get out, NOW" Tears were streaming down his face. He was broken and so was I. I opened the door and got out of his car. Before I could even turn around, he had reached over and slammed the car door shut. Connor's red Jetta was speeding out of sight.

I walked toward the trailer with some maniacal feeling of relief that the truth was out; some misguided confidence that I would be hearing from Connor tomorrow and talking this thing through. I still had some foolish hope that we would soon be married.

While I was taking a shower, putting on my nightgown, and getting into bed, Connor was heading back to Judd Street. He waited until Mary, Tory, Evan, and Andrew showed up, and then he went inside. They gathered in Tory's room and Connor, through tears and heartbreaking sobs, told them what happened, what I had done.

"Did you know, Mary, Tory? Did all of you know and just let me play the fool this whole time?"

"No, Connor, we didn't know," Tory assured. "Right, Mary? You didn't know did you?" she asked.

"No. Lucy never told me anything," Mary said.

Andrew began, "I did know that Pan loved Lucy. He wrote about her a lot in his journal but I didn't know they had been intimate like that. God, no, I didn't know, Connor. I'm so sorry."

"Well, I guess you know this changes things," Connor said. "It's been nice knowing you, but I can't...I won't be around here. I can't."

"Connor, just give it some time. Lucy loves you. She made a mistake but she loves you. Don't you believe that?" Mary pleaded for me.

"It doesn't matter now. It's just different for me now," Connor tried to explain as he hugged each of them. "She's not who I thought she was." And with that comment, Connor Hawthorn walked out of Judd Street and out of our lives.

CHAPTER 22

****

I wait for you to call me home
While waiting, thoughts I often roam
Like words I need to say to you
Mistakes that I cannot undo
To look at you and melt again
I think about what might have been
Forced to hold this bitter end
And here I'll wait...forever?

I woke up the next morning feeling strangely calm and well-rested considering the trauma I had endured just hours before. I felt relieved, like the air had cleared between Connor and me. There were no secrets between us anymore so we could just move past all the negativity and carry on with life as planned. I felt light and energized as I emerged from my tiny bedroom and went to the kitchen for a bowl of Capt'n Crunch in chocolate milk, one of Connor's indulgent creations. Mom and Dad had already gone to their Saturday morning breakfast spot so I sat on the couch and mindlessly watched cartoons. I was waiting for his red Jetta to pull up or for the phone to ring, neither of which ever happened.

A car did eventually pull up but it was the silver station wagon. Mary, Tory, and Andrew had come all the way across town to see how I was doing. They also needed to have a talk with me. At this point, I didn't know about Connor's late-night visit to Judd Street, but boy was I about to find out.

Andrew pulled a kitchen chair into the living room while Mary and Tory joined me on the couch. He wasted no time, "So you had sex with Pan?"

"God, Andrew, don't beat around the bush or anything," I replied a little annoyed at the way he tossed my dirty laundry around.

"Well, it's probably easier to hear about it from me than from Connor's friend in the middle of Nevo I presume. That was quite a show last night." Mary and Tory looked at me with accusing eyes. My light and happy demeanor diminished, brutalized from the assault.

"Look, Connor knows now and there are no more secrets between us. I don't know what else to tell you except that it was a mistake and I'm sorry. Connor is going to forgive me; he just needs some time."

"Connor is over it. He came to Judd Street last night and told us goodbye, Lucy. This is not just going to go away," Mary said. She informed me of their conversation in Tory's room and how he walked out after saying, "It's been nice knowing you" and "She's not who I thought she was."

"Mary, Tory, Andrew...listen to me. I know that Connor is shocked and hurt right now but you don't know him like I do. You don't know us like I do. There is no way we are over," I said getting up from the couch. I went into my room and for the first time since I had hidden it away, I slipped my engagement ring to Connor onto my finger. I walked back out into the living room and showed them, "See, we are getting married and I will go with him to Georgia if that's what he wants." Mary and Tory didn't know if they should laugh with excitement or cry from disappointment. Andrew shook his head at me accusingly.

"Well, honey, you just need to go put that ring right back where you've been hiding it. Connor is gone," he said matter-of-factly. He was not one to perpetuate lies or encourage delusions. As he stood up indicating he was ready to leave, he said, "You need to go ahead and let Chapel Hill know you plan to be there in August. You cannot let that opportunity pass you by while you wait around here for someone who is already gone."

"Andrew, could you be any more brutal?" I asked holding my stomach, suddenly feeling sick.

He walked over to me, cupped my chin in his hand, kissed my forehead, and said, "It's only because I care about you. Let's go girls. I've got a job to get to." Mary and Tory looked almost as distressed as I did as they hugged me and followed Andrew out the door.

I sat right back down on the couch wearing my engagement ring. He was going to call or show up, and I was going to be ready. I refused to believe that we could be over because of one mistake. Connor Hawthorn was mine; and I was his - completely. He couldn't just forget me like that. How could he just not love me anymore? He will call or come here. Connor will come back and I'll be ready. I'll be ready when he comes back.

CHAPTER 23

****

What he meant to say...
So wrong
So lost
So out of love
So forgotten
No more feeling
No more healing
No more hating
Or hurting over you
Life goes on
And I do too.

I requested that my hours be increased at The Record Exchange because it was the one place I could be without succumbing to my emotions. I could not stand to be at home or on Judd Street or at Nevo because those places were marked too heavily by our recent history. When I was at home, I spent most of my time sitting at the kitchen table and I slept on the couch because I couldn't bear to go into my room.

Mom finally brought it up one evening, "So where has Connor

been these past couple of weeks?"

"Mom, I...he's...I don't know." I could not form the words. She understood and did not push for more information.

My dad simply replied, "Well I'll be a son of a bitch. She's run him off." What could I say, he was absolutely right. His comment made me realize that I wasn't the only one who had lost Connor.

"Do you want to go with us?" Mom asked as she and my dad were leaving to have dinner at K&W Cafeteria like they did every Friday evening at five o'clock.

"No thanks. I'm not really hungry," I said.

In blind desperation, as soon as they walked out, I called his barracks. "May I speak to Connor Hawthorn?"

"Who's calling?" a stern voice commanded.

"Um, Lucy Bells."

"Ma'am, Sergeant First Class Hawthorn is unavailable now and will continue to be unavailable. Please do not call this number again." The phone call ended. I felt sick. I was sick. I ran to the bathroom at the end of our narrow hall and threw up, and then dry heaved until I fell on the floor beside the toilet. I lay there exhausted, crying with every ounce of energy I had left until I fell asleep. No one came to wake me or to even see if I was alive.

I woke up early on Saturday morning and stepped into the shower. My body felt stiff and twisted from sleeping on the bathroom floor all night. While in the shower, I thought about how I should have taken driver's education instead of putting it off for two years to take extra study halls. That way I could just get in the car and speed away from this place that constantly reminded me of Connor. But no; I was eighteen and couldn't even drive. I never needed to before. I always had Connor. Now, I was stranded; marooned in a trailer park.

****

Connor made one more trip to Freedom Manor Mobile Home Park. He pulled his red Jetta around the cul-de-sac and parked along the edge of our corner lot one last time. I can only tell this part of the story from what my mom told me since I was at work on that Sunday afternoon. Mom answered the door. "Connor! I am so happy to see you. Where have you been?" Dad stood up as he always did when Connor came in to shake his hand. Mom said Connor seemed as if he was about to cry when he did not take Dad's hand but hugged him instead. Then he just said things had not worked out between us but would not give any explanation as to why.

"There is one thing in Lucy's room I need to get before I go. May I go in there, just for a minute?" Connor asked. Of course, they let him go. Mom said he stayed in there several minutes with the door closed and when he came out his eyes were red as if he had been crying. She did not see anything in his hands so she guessed whatever it was must have been in his pocket. She was right about that; it was my engagement ring. Mom and Dad never knew about our engagement since I had already become part of Connor's past before we could announce our big plans for the future. He shook my dad's hand now and hugged my mom. He walked out of the trailer and as prescribed by his DNA, did not look back.

I had one last act of desperation left in me. Mom and Dad were right there in the living room when I took a seat on a barstool and dialed the number to Connor's home in Savannah. Trudi answered.

"Trudi, it's Lucy. I'm calling because, well, I wanted to talk to you because, um. I guess I don't really know what I was going to say. I just want to talk about Connor. He won't talk to me. He's just gone."

"I know darlin'. I know what's been happening. He told me everything and I don't know what to tell you except that you should just try to get on with your life like he has. I don't agree with him bringing some girl he's just met home but he's grown and I can't tell him what to do."

"He's taking a girl there, to your house?" I said as my stomach began to turn sick at the thought of another girl sitting in my seat in his red Jetta, meeting his family, making love to him on the floor beside the squeaky bed like we had.

"Yes, they are coming here this weekend. Listen, honey, I know this is hard, but Connor is just like this. He had a girlfriend in high school that we all thought was really serious and then he just left her when he enlisted in the military. I guess he has a way of just letting go."

I was paralyzed. So many thoughts were running through my head. He has a new girlfriend. Did he give her my engagement ring? Maybe I was just not that special to him after all. No, that's crazy.

"I don't care what he did before he met me, Trudi. And I don't care about this rebound girl whoever she is. Connor and I have something special. Can't you talk to him?"

"I already have, darlin'. I don't want it to be this way, but I can't make decisions for him. He's a grown man. You had something special, I agree. But maybe he just needs some time. Right now, he seems happy and that's my main concern, Lucy. Hopefully, you understand. Just give him some time and if it's meant to be then it will be."

My mouth started to fill with pre-vomit saliva. I thought, "Here we go again." I dropped the phone and ran to the bathroom, making it just in time. I threw up until there was nothing left and once again fell over beside the toilet. My cries came out in uncontrollable loud heaves. I guess Mom finished the call but I never asked.

I don't remember how I made it to my bed, but that's where I woke up the next morning and immediately broke down into tears. What I would have given to look out of my window and see his red car parked along the cul-de-sac. I would have easily given my life to know in my last breath that he had forgiven me and that I wasn't just some horrible person who had irreparably broken her own life and Connor's heart. It seemed to me in the moment, however, that my life held such little value that it couldn't even be exchanged for his forgiveness.

Mom heard me and came into my room. She sat on the edge of my bed and said, "Don't give up hope on Connor. You two were something special no matter what happened. Nothing can kill your love if it was really true and sincere. Just don't give up hope on him. Things have a way of working themselves out." Even if I had known what to say, I could not respond. I got up and barely stumbled into the kitchen because I couldn't bear to be in my room.

Halfway through the week, Mom called the admissions office and confirmed my enrollment at UNC Chapel Hill. While she was making plans for my future, I was sitting behind the counter at The Record Exchange through a slow double shift. On the way home from work that evening, over a cheese quesadilla and a Diet Pepsi, Mom said, "Lucy, I called the university today and you're all set. You need to be ready to go in two weeks and it would be good to go ahead and let your manager know so he can hire a replacement." "Ok, Mom. I will. Thanks for doing that...for calling." I sat there numbly knowing that I would have to go on with my life, for now, without Connor. I was going to Chapel Hill alone and Connor was going home with another girl.

Maybe other couples can survive a bump in the road, even horrible bumps like infidelity and lies, but Connor was different. He did, after all, possess his grandfather's ability to look ahead and not back. He was able to move on and open himself to love again without regret. I, however, have never possessed any such qualities. I have always been stuck right there at that moment in time, holding on to the belief that we could never really end. I had to let him go and attempt to continue my life without him, but I always believed he would return to me one day just like my faithfully returning fireflies had when I was a little girl in my North Carolina backyard.

****

Over the next two weeks, life as I knew it began to squeeze me out. My parents talked openly of plans to tear down the wall that separated my room from Mary's old room to make space for an adjustable hospital bed for my dad. Mom expressed her desire to move his chair into the new space as well. Dad agreed as long as he got a new TV so he could watch CNN.

Even Judd Street was falling apart. Evan moved to New York to pursue his dreams as a photographer. Mary and Tory were moving to the mountains of North Carolina to work for friends of Tory's parents in a bakery. They would learn the business and then, hopefully, one day open a bakery of their own; not a very gothic path, I know. Andrew was the last resident of Judd Street to leave. He was moving to an apartment across town to live with his new lover.

The Record Exchange had no more use for me either. They hired a skater boy with dreads who drove an old beat-up Volkswagen Bus to take my place. He would fit right in since he, like the others, looked like he was born to work there.

Around noon on Sunday, while Mom was driving me to The Record Exchange to work my final shift training my replacement, I saw Connor one last time across a busy intersection. We were both turning left. His new girlfriend was in the passenger seat beside him. All I could see was her long, dark hair. I didn't say anything but my stomach felt sick. I focused my gaze straight ahead while Mom drove. Connor Hawthorn, the keeper of my heart, with another girl beside him, drove away from me in the opposite direction.

Yes, it certainly seemed that all my familiar people and places had squeezed me right out. There was no more room for me to live in my hometown. All of a sudden, a college campus was just what I needed; a new start, a new horizon, an old plan. I was right back to the old Lucy, the solitary girl who avoided attention and just wanted to get out of that town.

CHAPTER 24

****

"…He who is fixed to a star
does not change his mind."
-Leonardo Da Vinci

I dropped my bags and boxes and plopped down on the single bed closest to the door. There was another bed across the tiny dorm room but I had not been assigned a roommate yet, so for now it was all mine. Mom walked in behind me and sat down in the chair next to my desk. "Well, here we are; your new home for the next few years."

"Yeah, I guess. I just always imagined this moment so differently. I thought I would be more excited, you know."

"Lucy, you have been through a lot. Just give it time. You'll meet some new people and eventually all that sadness you are carrying right now will disappear. Just trust me."

"Hmm, that sounds a little unrealistic, but I'm here, so I'll try to make the best of it."

We finished unloading my few belongings from the car except for my records and tapes because I couldn't bear to listen to music anymore. I said goodbye to my mom, and then tears streamed down my face as she drove away. I felt alone and unprepared to fend for myself. I was still that shy, socially awkward, broken-hearted girl after all. I didn't have Mary's social skills to use or Connor to break down my walls and now not even Morrissey could commiserate with me. I didn't have my old familiar places to hide. I wiped my tears and hesitantly set out across a busy college campus in search of something, anything new.

An unfamiliar scent filled the air as I approached a bustling little street on the edge of campus lined with restaurants, bars, and stores filled to the brim with college gear. I found the source of the smell in a coffee shop. It was coming from the beans that were roasting right there in the front of the store. I ordered a cup and found a corner table, reverting back to that misfit on Judd Street in the corner chair who observed life but didn't really participate in it. I sat there for a while watching people come and go, new friendships being forged, old friends reuniting, couples looking into each other's eyes, loners like me reading or writing. I sort of hoped, against every fiber in my being, that one of those strangers would pluck me out of my corner and introduce me to a world I never imagined like Connor had done.

I quickly became a regular at Judge's House of Coffee. Every day, after my classes, I would go there to study and further my growing dependence on caffeine. Unlike when I was in high school, I actually had to study to make good grades; a humbling academic realization. I would stack my books and get lost in them for a couple of hours before walking back across campus to my lonely dorm room where the studying would often continue. My first semester went pretty much like that: class,

Judge's, dorm.

I had to consciously block out thoughts about Connor because the pain they caused was too severe. I had already cried myself to sleep for too many nights (thank God I didn't have a roommate). But it didn't stop there. I was crying through every shower and I still couldn't eat properly without feeling nauseated. I even had to walk out of a few class sessions when thoughts of him shoved their way in. I wondered if he squeezed her fingertips like he did mine. I wondered if he ever slipped up and called her Lucy. I knew deep down inside he would forgive me and want me again. I think I was just biding my time until then. In the meantime though, all I needed to do was survive.

By the time my second semester arrived, I felt slightly more at home in the little college town I had come to love. I still had a dorm room to myself and my corner table at my favorite coffee shop that filled the town with the exotic scent of roasting coffee. I had not made any new friends yet but that was typical. There were, however, a few people who recognized me around the dorm and at Judge's. One evening when I was returning to the dorm, one of those acquaintances did more than just say "hi", she actually stopped me to talk. "Hey, I'm Ashley. I live on the hall below you and I always see you coming and going by yourself."

"Yeah, hi, Lucy Bells. I mostly am by myself. It's okay though, you know. I'm just sort of like that."

"Well, we should hang out sometime...get to know each other."

"Yeah, okay, sometime. Sure," I said not really thinking it would ever happen.

"See you soon then," she said and continued on her way.

Why did socializing freak me out so badly? I wanted to get better at it so I became determined to follow up with Ashley's invitation.

We met at Judge's on a Friday night for coffee. It felt strange sitting at my corner table with no pile of books to hide behind, only two cofffee mugs and an actual person sitting across from me wanting to talk. Ashley was pretty by anyone's standards, way more striking than average. She had a fair, perfect complexion and dark brown eyes. Her blonde hair fell in layered waves around her delicate face and onto her narrow shoulders. She was taller than me and skinnier but somehow managed to grow large breasts. I wondered why some people won the lottery on looks and others of us just got by. I hoped she would do most of the talking because I was ill-prepared and didn't want to break down in public over Connor if that story should begin to spill out of me. So I began asking questions: Where are you from? What are you studying? What kind of music do you listen to? I wondered if she felt like she was being interviewed. This wasn't so bad. I relaxed and let down my guard a little. I told her that I was an education major and a recovering heartbreak victim just to keep the conversation flowing. She seemed to understand, possibly having her own version of some sordid love affair. Neither of us delved too deeply into those waters. After our first social interaction, Ashley and I would meet sometimes for coffee and she visited me in my dorm room pretty regularly. We talked about current things like our classes and her lively social life, but never much more than that. My history was too wrought with pain, too twisted up with drama. I couldn't unload that on anyone.

Judge's was sort of like another version of Judd Street for me, like a portal moving me toward different experiences. I spent time there just sitting back and making observations of people living their lives. It was like I existed behind a two-way mirror and no one saw me, yet I could see them interacting and connecting. I began to feel an insatiable need for human contact. Judge's, like Judd Street, brought it to me in the form of a boy.

He sat right down, uninvited, across from me and moved my stack of textbooks to the side so they were not directly between us. His skin was tan and freckled, his eyes were blue and his short curls were dark brown. He was dressed in faded jeans and a Beatles t-shirt worn thin. With a strong accent that sounded strangely British, he began just above a whisper, "I'm a journalism major but I really want to write poetry and play guitar in my band for a living. What do you reallllly want to do?"

His intensity was a little startling. My face was already red with the embarrassment of social interaction. I was shocked by his presence at my table and by his apparent interest in me. I, of course, fumbled over my words, "I'm going to be a teacher, I think, but I'm not sure what else beyond that. I don't know." I looked at the coffee cup in front of me to keep from looking at him and wondered why I was born so inept at conversation.

"A teacher. I admire you already. So, what is your name?"

"Lucy," I said still looking down.

"Beautiful," he said and then paused. "My...my name is Henry in case you wanted to know. I mean, you didn't ask, but there it is anyway."

I looked up now, smiled and shook my head. I offered my hand to shake over our cups of coffee and said, "Well, Henry, thank you for telling me. I would have asked though. So, where are you from? I can't really place your accent."

"I'm from South Africa. I'm here on a student visa to get a more worldly experience as part of my education." While he was talking to me about his reasons for being here, my mind shifted to Connor. I wished for it to be him across from me talking to me and showing interest in me. I believed that if he and I were in the same room, our connection would be too strong to ignore; we were so perfectly paired. I halfway listened to Henry, nodding and smiling.

Like an involuntary and unstoppable curse over my body, I yawned. I tried to stop it but that was futile.

"Oh God, I'm boring you," he said in response.

"No, not at all. That's embarrassing; sorry about that. I'm just really tired. Honestly, I'm enjoying your conversation so much," I said trying hard to be polite and apologetic.

"Well then, maybe I should I just walk you home so that you can rest. I wouldn't want you falling asleep at my show tonight," he said smiling.

"What do you mean?" I asked.

"I want you to come tonight, as my guest, to The Local. My band is playing. We play soulful rock fucking awesome covers. I think you'll like it. It's an acoustic set tonight so we won't blast your ears. Will you come, Lucy?"

"I've never been to The Local but I know where it is. It's just up the street a little, right?"

"Yes, so you're coming. Come on, let's get you home. Let me see; it's three o'clock right now so that only gives you eight hours. We'll start playing around eleven. Come on. Come on," he urged.

This was all so strange. As we walked across campus together, it seemed that everyone knew Henry. People were calling out hellos from left and right.

"You're really popular, it seems," I said.

"I know; it's the accent. People just want to hear me talk all the time. I don't get it," he said and then winked. We made it to my dorm and he offered to carry my books up to my room for me but I said that I could manage.

"It was nice to meet you and thanks for walking with me."

"I'll see you tonight, Lucy. Promise me. I'll break down on stage if I come out and you're not sitting there to cheer me on. Promise me."

"Okay, I promise. I'll try to come."

"Oh wow, you'll try. That's not good enough."

"I promise I'll come."

"Now that's better." He leaned in and kissed my cheek. "See you tonight, Lucy. You promised," Henry said as he backed away from me...pointing at me. I was just standing there shell-shocked at this whole experience. He turned around and trotted away. What the hell just happened? Who was this person? Why me?

I walked up to my room and laid down on my bed. I didn't think about my new friend, I thought about Connor. I wondered what he was doing at that moment; if he had thought about me when I turned nineteen last month, if he was happier with her than he was with me, if he thought of me when they made love. I drifted off into a dreamless sleep.

I woke up with a jolt and had the vaguest memory of a boy walking me home. For a second, I thought I might have dreamed it but then my memory cleared. I looked over at the digital clock which read 10:47pm. "Am I seriously thinking about going to this place tonight? What the hell is happening to me?"

My mind was spinning as I quickly pulled on my jeans, changed into a black t-shirt, brushed my teeth, and pulled my hair back into a ponytail. I was on my way out of the door when the clock changed to 10:53pm.

"Okay, that was fast," I said closing the door behind me. I had no idea what to expect. I needed this though. It was going to be like therapy or like an experiment to see if I could let someone else, anyone else in. I crossed campus in record time and, for the first time, opened the black door to The Local.

I walked into the dark room. There was a bar to my left. It was already lined with people sitting on stools. Small tables were haphazardly placed about. Most of them were already surrounded by people sitting in chairs. There were several people standing in front of the little stage where Henry's band had already begun to play. I walked toward the stage but stayed close to the wall, in the shadows. I saw Henry sitting on a little stool playing his guitar. Three other boys were on stage with him: a singer, a drummer, and a bassist. Their music was laid back and the vocals sounded very...independent. Not all together terrible. I leaned against the wall and watched what was happening inside The Local on this random Thursday evening.

Eventually, Henry spied me. He smiled and his entire demeanor seemed to change. During their next break, he came over to me and said, "I didn't think you were coming. When I came out here and you were nowhere in sight, I thought I was going to end it all and just fling myself off the stage to my death."

"Okay, that would have been a little dramatic," I replied.

"Lucy, I'm glad that you came," he said and then leaned in for another kiss on the cheek.

"Me too," I said, thinking I could do this; that this wasn't so bad.

"We have three more songs before another band plays. Here, sit here," he said pulling aside two chairs, "and keep this one for me. I'll be back."

When his band was finished playing, he made his way through high fives, handshakes, and pats on the back to where I was sitting. "I am very impressed," I said.

"Well, thanks. We've been playing together for about six months but individually, we've been playing music our whole lives. It's what I love to do. For now, it's just for fun, you know. Do you want to get out of here?" he asked out of the blue.

"What? You mean you want to leave now?" I said a little confused by his spontaneity.

"Yes, with you. I want to leave with you."

"Okay. Sure. Where should we go?" I asked naively.

"I have an idea," Henry responded. "You don't have a roommate and I do. I think your place would be perfect."

I got it. He just wanted to go someplace and have sex. How typical. I began to think how it had really been a long time. Maybe I needed to do this just as part of my experiment even though the last time I had sex with someone other than Connor, he killed himself. Maybe I should tread cautiously or maybe I should just stop thinking so damn much.

"Let's go," I said grabbing his hand.

We took our time walking across campus which gave us an opportunity to talk. I found out that he played rugby, loved classical music, jazz, and rock and roll. He had been playing piano since he was seven and guitar since he was twelve. He turned twenty just before the New Year and would be here until the end of the semester. Then he'd return to South Africa for a year, graduate, and begin his career as a field journalist, a reporter...a writer.

"Fascinating," I replied after hearing his plans so perfectly laid out.

"Yes. But I'm afraid all I really want to do is write songs and play my guitar for the likes of you," he said grabbing my hand and rushing us along the last few steps.

When we entered my room, he looked around like a detective trying to find information. He sat at my desk and flipped through my books, notebooks, picture, etc. "What are you looking for," I finally said, kicked back on my little bed.

"Something, anything that will give me insight into who you are. You speak so few words and I speak too many."

"I'm Lucy Bells, future college professor. For now, that's enough, right?"

"Yes, I suppose it is," Henry said, now looking straight at me. He took two steps forward and sat beside me on the bed. He leaned toward me and kissed my lips. I kissed him back. I wondered if he could sense my hesitation and sadness. He scooted closer to me and put his hands around my waist. He began taking off my shirt but I wouldn't let him. "What's wrong?" he asked. "Don't you want me?"

"Yes, I mean, I don't know. I do, but I'm..." Henry kissed me and became more aggressive, trying to hurry things along before I completely backed out.

But he was too late. I couldn't do it. I stood up. "Henry, I'm sorry. I can't. You're welcome to stay for a while and talk, but I can't do this. Not right now. I'm sorry you came all the way here for nothing."

He didn't say anything right away. I thought he was going to be angry and curse at me while storming out. To my surprise, he said, "I am disappointed, but only in myself for being such a boorish asshole. I am the one who is sorry, Lucy. I am not mad at you." He stood up and hugged me, genuinely...tightly for a minute at least. "I'm going to go now. I fear I've put you through enough this evening."

"No, really, it's okay," I said relieved.

"We will meet again, if only for coffee. Thank you for keeping your promise and your virtue tonight, Dearest Lucy Bells. You're different from other girls and I mean that as a compliment." He kissed my cheek this time and walked out of my dorm room taking care to close the door slowly, gently. Henry was great. He was nice, interesting, talented, sexy, and had a foreign accent to top it all off; if not him, then who? I fell back on my little bed knowing that I still undoubtedly belonged to Connor whether he wanted me or not. Right then I became fully aware that my college experience would not consist of the normal partying and one night stands. Thank God.

CHAPTER 25

****

"When one door closes, another one opens;
but we often look so long and so regretfully
upon the closed door that we do not see
the one which has opened for us."

- Alexander Graham Bell

My first year of college came to an end in June. I sat in Judge's with a blank greeting card and a large mug of fresh roasted coffee and began to craft my thoughts:

Dear Trudi,

My first year at UNC has been quite an experience. I am proud to say I received excellent grades except for one C in a logic course (I still can't figure out why I needed that one anyway). Living away from home has been different yet liberating. It became very difficult for me to be there after Connor left...well, honestly, it became difficult for me to be anywhere. A change of scenery and routines was necessary.

I am studying to become a teacher and eventually a college professor. I like the thoughts of being on a college campus for years to come. It suits me. Guess what! I can drive now! I took a driver's education class last semester and have passed my driving exam. Connor would be surprised, I'm sure.

I hope your family is well. Please keep me informed about Connor. I know we are no longer together, but I still care for him deeply and would like to know that he is happy and healthy. Where is he? What is he doing now that his military service has ended? Don't worry, I am better. Time and distance have worked their magic on my broken heart.

Thinking of you,

Lucy

"Good thing I'm a better liar when I write," I thought to myself while finalizing my card and addressing the envelope. Now I would just have to wait to see if Trudi was willing to keep me in her circle.

During the summer months, I took a couple of courses so that I could remain on campus. I also found a job. Ashley, who also stayed on campus during the summer, was a waitress at a busy pizza dive. She came up to my room one evening and said, "There's a job opening at the restaurant where I work. You should come apply."

"I have no experience. I've only worked at a record store." I replied a little amused at the thought of me attempting to be a waitress.

"Just come. If I can do it, so can you. And it's a great way to meet people...well, boys, but you knew what I meant. Come on. Get ready and let's go." She was right. I needed a new experience. No one except Ashley had come into my room since Henry. Maybe I was ready to work on that social experiment again. Maybe distance and time had worked their magic.

"Yeah, you're right. I can probably do this. Let's go."

I was hired on the spot. It didn't take too long for me to learn how to serve pizza and it was nice to have a little extra cash. Unlike Ashley, I didn't use my job as an outlet to meet boys. Anyway, it was like I had the word "Taken" tattooed on my forehead. No one since Henry had even shown an interest in me. I found out that distance and time had not lessened my conviction for Connor. I still believed he would call or show up to right this wrong and I was going to be ready when that happened. So I didn't show interest in anyone either. In fact, even if someone had hit on me, they would have been in for a rude awakening, like poor Henry. I still missed Connor too much to let anyone near me. I missed the way he smelled, his green eyes, the way he squeezed my fingertips, and his hard beautiful body. I especially missed his soft, deep voice reassuring me of his love even though I never felt like I deserved it. No one could replace him or even come close.

With only one week left before my second year of college began, I walked quickly back to my dorm room with a very important correspondence clutched tightly in my hand and pressed firmly to my chest. I guess Trudi did want to keep me in her circle after all since she replied to my card. My hands were shaking as I pulled the little card with a rabbit on the front from the envelope.

Dearest Lucy,

I am so glad to hear you are enjoying college life. You have done such a great job. I'm very proud of you and I know your parents are too.

Mama is still living with us because I just can't let her go to a senior home. She continues to grieve Daddy's passing, but we all still do. Everyone else is doing just great.

I am going to be honest with you about Connor because you told me you could handle it without getting upset. He is married to the girl he brought home and they are living in Atlanta in an apartment. No real wedding. They just went to the courthouse and did it without any of us knowing. Both of them are working in restaurants but Connor has enrolled in college and is about to start classes this fall. To be honest, Lucy, I don't like it. I don't really like her. I think I'm always comparing her to you and that's not fair. You have to go on and live your life to the fullest. It sounds like you are doing just that. Is there someone special yet or are you too busy for that?

Please keep in touch with me. I want to know how your life progresses.

Love always,

Trudi

I had lied to her in my card so I deserved this. Any sort of bliss I was experiencing from my ignorance about Connor's life had been extinguished by Trudi's words. I read the last paragraph over to really absorb it; "I am going to be honest with you about Connor..." I lay back and tried to concentrate on breathing, in through my nose and out through my mouth while tears streamed down my face creating big wet circles on my pillow. My heart was beating fast and my head was burning hot. Connor was married. My sick mind went right to the part where he looked in her eyes and said, "I do." I imagined the kiss they shared, wondered if they had a wedding cake, did they have a first dance and if so, to what song...and on and on. It turns out that lying, even in writing, was not meant for me. Neither time nor distance had rendered any healing whatsoever upon my heart. It still belonged to Connor. I fell into a deep, coma-like sleep for hours. I believe it was a gift from God; an escape without dying.

I woke up with a bad idea in my aching head and Trudi's card in my clenched fist. It was dark in my room and the digital clock was glowing in big red numbers, 11:37pm. I got up, took off my jeans and sweatshirt and slipped on my black sundress, black boots, black sweater, red lip gloss. I let down my ponytail so my hair could hang loose and crossed campus like a zombie looking for something, anything to help me forget. I found The Local and opened the black door for the second time.

I wasn't a drinker, but I thought tonight, if ever in my life, I should drink. I headed confidently to the bar and stood there feeling awkward until the bartender glanced my way. He hurried over and said, "What'll it be, hun?" I didn't know what to say. I had no answer - no idea what to order. I wasn't even of age, but I don't think anyone cared. After a few seconds, he raised his eyebrows and said, "Is everything ok, darlin'?" I replied, "Honestly, I just need something strong...I don't know anything about liquor." "I got you. Stay right there." He returned with two shot glasses and a bottle of amber-colored liquid. He sat the glasses on the bar and filled each one. "Two shots of Tennessee Whiskey, on the house. This should do the trick, baby girl." I took one glass in each hand and downed the one in my right first...then my left. I slammed both glasses back on the bar at the same time and gasped for air. "Let it settle...come get me if you need anything. Name's Jay. Now go forget whatever it is need's forgettin'."

I wasn't drawn to the shadows tonight. An acoustic band was playing. They seemed to be more experienced and more popular than Henry's band. The little tables and chairs had all been pushed aside and the large crowd stood facing the stage; everyone swaying and dancing in place. I don't really know how to describe what I was feeling except for numb. That's the only word that comes to mind as I recall slinking my way into the smoky crowd and trying to feel the music, to feel anything.

Two, maybe three, songs were played before he put a cold, wet bottle in my hand and then held his up for a toast. Our bottles clinked. He leaned down and said, "What's your name? I've never seen you here before."

"Lucy. Thanks for the beer," I said taking a swig and thinking how it didn't taste as horrible as it had when I was sixteen. It actually soothed the sting two shots of whiskey had left in my throat.

"I'm Jason. Nice to meet you, Lucy." We smiled at each other and then stood there swaying with the crowd to the guitars and piano. Another beer was handed to me and I drank it feeling its effects come over me like a weight being lifted from my existence. Another beer...another weight; one more beer, one more weight. I felt like I was floating in his arms. His hands were around my waist, mine were on his arms. We swayed while our bodies pushed against each other's. It felt good to be held, to be light and carefree if just for that moment.

Not much time passed before his hand lifted my chin and our lips met. Jason tried to pull away but I took it deeper, getting my tongue involved. He was ready and willing. We made out surrounded by a crowd, and I couldn't have cared less. He broke from our deep kiss and said, "Let's go sit down. I need to get to know you a little better." I giggled and tried to kiss him again. This was so dangerous but I really didn't care. I wanted to be someone else, not the girl Connor had forgotten. I wanted to do things Lucy would never do.

We sat next to the wall in chairs facing each other. All I knew so far was that he was much taller than me and had shaggy dark hair and thick, soft lips. I took a second and tried to focus on the man I had just kissed. Though it was difficult with my wondering eyes and spinning mind, I could see that his body was big and strong. He looked older than regular college guys, handsome and confident. "So what do you want to know?" I began. He chuckled, showing off his charming smile. Maybe my drunkenness was endearing to him.

"Okay. I want to know if you are a student."

"That's easy, yes."

"Are you new or have you been here a while?"

"A while," I responded laughing for no reason.

"Where are your friends? Where is your boyfriend?"

"Please no," I said shaking my head. I stood up and straddled his lap facing him. I leaned onto his shoulder and whispered in his ear, "Take me somewhere beautiful."

I guess, since I was drunk, I could think about Connor without it causing me intolerable pain. In my imagination, I was holding his hand, falling back onto a patch of cool grass by a rushing creek, watching the navy sky turn to sparkling black velvet. We walked out of The Local together...me holding onto his arm, smiling deliriously at the sweet memory flooding my mind. I was there, under the stars, as I slid to the middle seat in a stranger's car. I laid my head on his arm. For a moment it was Connor. He drove while I just sat there and smiled.

He carried me inside a house that smelled of incense and clove cigarettes. I breathed in deeply taking in all the Judd Street nostalgia. He laid me on the couch. I could smell coffee brewing just before I lost consciousness. I soon woke up and grabbed my head because it was still spinning and I still felt like laughing for no apparent reason. I must have been out for only a few minutes because it was still dark in the house, and my mind and body were still buzzing from the two shots and four beers I had gulped down at The Local. He was sitting on the couch with my legs on his lap playing a video game. "Well, hello, stranger. I fixed you some coffee but you decided to nap first."

"I don't really think I decided to nap; it just sort of happened. Sorry."

"Don't worry. It's all good."

"Thanks. I am so embarrassed. God, I'm sorry. Thanks for being so...um...honorable, I guess." He looked at me and chuckled. "If it's not too much trouble, I could really use a cup of that coffee. It smells amazing."

"Sure thing...and it's still hot. Are you hungry?" he asked as he stood up from the couch. I noticed how tall and big he was.

"No, I can't think about eating right now."

He returned with the coffee and sat down beside me. He leaned over close to me after I had taken a careful sip or two. I thought about how Connor and I were so perfectly paired; he wasn't this much taller than me and his body didn't dwarf mine like this guy's did.

My thoughts were shifting back to the old Lucy. I had to get rid of her so I sat my coffee on the table, turned toward this large man and said, "I need you to know right now that I cannot remember your name but I really, really want to. I'm Lucy Bells and you are...?" I said holding out my hand for a shake.

"Jason. My name is Jason Watts and you are at my house three blocks from The Local. I'm a graduate student in computer science and I tutor students; just basically hang out on campus during the summer. Oh, I'm from Raleigh; lived around here all my life," he said shaking my hand the whole time.

I wanted him so badly right then. I grabbed his t-shirt, leaned back on the couch and pulled him with me. I closed my eyes. I wanted him to take control and he did. We shifted so that his big body covered my small body on the couch. "Are you sure you're okay with this? You don't know me, you know." He said between kisses.

"Shut up," I whispered.

When I woke up, it was light outside but his blinds and curtains were closed. I slipped over closer to him to get a better look in the dim light. I saw tattoos on his back and upper arms and a couple of scars on his side. His body was so big. I carefully slid to the edge of the bed and tiptoed into the bathroom just a few steps away. I whispered, "Thank God," because it was clean and not disgusting.

Unfortunately, the old Lucy was back. I broke down crying silently while I sat on the toilet. What had I just done with this stranger? Connor was so far from me right now. He had moved on and here I was trying to move on as well. What about the magic behind the message? I needed to be ready when he came back. And he would come back to me if I just kept surviving and praying. "Dear God, Please forgive me. I am so sorry and ashamed. Please bring Connor back to me. This is not who I am. Please bring Connor back. I don't know how to go on without him."

I washed my hands, splashed a little cold water on my face, and fixed my hair in a ponytail. While I gathered my belongings, I was relieved to see signs of protection; three little square packages scattered on the floor and ripped open. I had been too drunk to even ask...so stupid. Just short of closing the front door behind me, I turned and headed into the kitchen looking for a pen and piece of paper to leave a little note so he wouldn't think too lowly of me. I began writing, "Jason, Thanks for a wonderf..." then I scratched it out and wrote, "That was amazing. Call me" and put down my dorm number because Lucy would not have done that. I couldn't carry her sadness today after all. I was too exhausted from last night's alcohol-fueled activities to shoulder her burdens so I tried to be the girl who didn't care anymore.

I walked back to campus and then to my dorm feeling too sore to move. The crumpled card with the rabbit on the front was still there on my bed. "You've got to go," I said out loud shoving it deep in my desk drawer. I took a quick shower and got dressed for serving pizza. I had to be there at five. "Homework for two hours and a nap for one; I can do this."

****

"I knew I recognized you from somewhere," Jason said after I passed a bench where he was sitting on my way home from work. He fell in beside me.

"Oh, hi, Jason," I said now realizing that I had walked right past him without even so much as a glance. "I didn't see you there."

"So, you've served me pizza before. Did you know that?"

"Well, I've served a lot of pizza, so I don't doubt it," I replied laughing a little.

After a few quiet steps he said, "Hey, I want to see you again. I'd like to, um...you know, see you again."

"Well, here I am," I said playing dumb and trying not to seem trampy.

Then Jason proposed an idea, "Hey, let's go get a cup of coffee and get to know a little more about each other if you're not too tired. I mean I know you had a late night and just got off work but whaddaya say? I'll buy."

I stopped walking, thought for a moment and then replied, "Okay. I guess I can do that."

"Great, I know this little place where it won't be too crowded. Let's go this way." We walked a little while on campus until we came to a set of brick steps leading down to a door sort of hidden from sight, like an entrance to the basement of a building. The atmosphere was dark and quiet. A few people were sitting around with coffee mugs talking while Mazzy Star's laid back vocals crooned, "fade into you." He led me to a corner table and then ordered our coffee. "So maybe we got off on the wrong foot last night," Jason began.

I looked at him and shrugged, "Really, I don't know. Was it that bad?"

"God, no, I don't mean that. I just don't want you to think that's what I'm about; picking up girls at The Local and taking them back to my house. Last night was not my usual...you know, I don't normally..."

"It's okay. I was there too, remember; a willing participant. It's not my M.O. either, to be honest. I was upset and wanted to forget myself. I probably owe you a 'thanks' for helping me out with that and an apology for...well, everything else."

"Okay. Well, you're welcome and I don't accept your apology because you have no reason to be sorry. You want to talk to me about it, whatever it is you're trying to shake? I think you'll find that listening is among my many talents."

He looked at me so sincerely, like he really wanted to know what I was about. Did I dare begin telling Jason about Connor and me? No, I couldn't. It was too precious, too painful; not the kind of thing you just unload on a stranger, even if it was a stranger who knew me intimately. "I'm just, I don't know, a little stressed right now. You know, school, relationships, life..."

"Well, Lucy, are you in a relationship with someone right now? I'm not about to start World War III here am I? I don't want to cause trouble for you." Truthfully, I was still in a relationship with Connor even if he was married to someone else. I was desperately clutching this dream and would not let go. I could not let go of Connor. The thought was terrifying and anyway, he was coming back and I was going to be ready.

"Jason, it's complicated because I still...well, I am...never mind. I'm such an idiot. In my head I know I have to move on but emotionally...I'm kinda stuck."

"Been there, babe, but it gets better, well, easier as time goes on. Look, I'm willing to be a distraction if you'll let me," he said as he reached over and tucked a few fallen hairs behind my ear. That made me think about how I had once been a distraction for Connor but that was so different. Here was this gorgeous man wanting and willing to distract me from my heartache but I was too afraid to let go of it. I had to wait for Connor because it was coded in my DNA, written in my stars, flowing through my veins. I wasn't sure how to be Lucy Bells without him.

But I had kept Jason waiting long enough. The voice in my head was scolding, "Answer him, damn it. A distraction is what you need. Let Jason be the answer. Connor had no problem finding another distraction to replace your ass. DO IT!"

"OKAY!" I blurted out of nowhere. "Sorry, didn't mean to...I meant, just okay. Let's see how this works." I took one of his big hands in mine. He didn't squeeze my fingertips or cup my hands between his like Connor did. I was painfully aware that no one could ever replace him. But a break from my heartache might be nice once in a while. "I think I can handle a little distraction," I finally said.

"Whew. I seriously thought you were about to bust my bubble all over this little coffee shop. So, how about a little distraction tonight before you go to bed? Just putting it out there."

"I can't. I have too much to do tomorrow. School's about to start next week. I need to try and get some sleep and stay focused," I said, trying to stay true to Lucy and Connor.

"Well, I'm walking you home and I'm not asking."

"Well, okay then, I won't bother saying, 'no'. Let's go," I said, thinking how I really liked him, his personality, his big tattooed body, the way he was pursuing me.

On the way across campus, Jason told me that he was twenty-five and would be finishing grad school after this year. He had already been hired to work in Seattle with some computer graphics company. It all sounded very impressive. In fact, my usual heavy spirit was becoming light and a little euphoric the more he talked. Jason was an older man (by my nineteen year old standards) and had real plans. Even without liquid courage in cold wet bottles, I was feeling attracted to him.

"This is it. My dorm room is right up those steps. Maybe you could just come up for a minute. It's okay if you want to," I said, trying to be coy about my change of heart.

"Nope. You need to get a good start next week and I'm not going to be the reason if you don't." He leaned over and lifted my chin. He kissed me with closed lips, and then again, and then again. "I'll be at The Local this weekend. I'll be waiting for you." Jason winked at me and walked away. "God, I have to get myself together," I thought as I stood there too long wishing he would look back. He didn't.

A few minutes passed before I heard a knock on my door. I just knew it was Jason. I opened the door only to meet Ashley standing there with huge eyes peering at me. "Was that Jason Watts who just walked you home and kissed you on the lips? Oh my God! Tell me everything!" she blurted out.

"Why? Do you know him or something?" I asked just a little confused.

"Lucy, you really need to get out more. He is the hottest grad student on this campus and he is brilliant. He tutors computer graphics students like me but I've never had the good fortune to be in one of his sessions. He has already designed and sold like a bunch of video games. He's independently wealthy and hasn't even graduated yet. How did you meet him? What the hell is going on here?"

"I just met him last night...no big deal, really," I said trying to leave out the part where I got drunk and let him have his way with me.

"Well, make it a big deal because he's worth it. God, I'm so freaking jealous right now. If you fuck him you have to spill. I'm not even playing."

"Watch your mouth. And I'll consider it," I said conveniently leaving out the part where I already had.

"Oh, you will. Trust me. I've got to get back to the less appealing boy waiting in my room." Ashley kissed my cheek and left, closing the door behind her.

"Well, it's a good thing he didn't come up here tonight. We certainly would not have been alone," I thought to myself.

My first week back to a full semester of classes was busy,

and I was thankful for the lack of free time. From morning to late afternoon I was either in class, at the library, or at Judge's studying. Then at night, I went to work serving pizza. Friday night was the first night I had off during the week. I felt conflicted about what I should do as I sat on my little bed watching the red numbers on my digital clock climb higher: 11:15pm, 11:16pm...11:27pm. One part of me wanted to bury my head in my pillow, unleash my raw, suppressed emotions and cry my eyes out over Connor. Another part of me wanted to feel nothing. I took the easy way out, pulled on another sundress, let my ponytail down, and made determined strides in my black heels toward The Local.

I opened the black door for the third time. A rock and roll band was playing, plugged in and loud. The atmosphere was busy, smoky, and smelled heavily of beer. Trying to act nonchalant, like I wasn't nervous and obviously out of my element, I approached the crowd and worked my way in; really just taking cover, trying to hide. Jason was not there as I looked around, at the bar, along the walls. I came up with a plan: two more songs and if Jason hasn't found me, I'm leaving. Two songs later, I was heading toward the black door.

I walked back to my dorm preparing to unleash the raw emotions I had opted against earlier in the evening. I was imagining Connor holding my hand and squeezing my fingertips, laughing in his high pitched way, knowing everything about me, my family, my faults, my issues and loving me anyway. No one could ever know me like he did. Anyone else would always be a stranger compared to the depths of Connor and Lucy. And he would come back to me. I was sure of that.

My distraction came just in time, just before the flood gates broke and the tears started to flow. As I approached the sidewalk leading up to my dorm, I heard a voice say, "I like those heels, Miss Bells." My heart dropped to the bottom of my stomach; no one called me "Miss Bells" except Connor. I stopped short of one more step and turned around just before Jason swept me off my feet, literally. I felt like I was ten feet in the air as he carried me like this toward my dorm.

"Jason, turn around and just keep walking in the other direction. We can't stay here," I said remembering Ashley and here peeping eyes.

"Yes ma'am," Jason said as he made an abrupt turn on the sidewalk.

"Where were you? I got all dressed up and went to The Local but no Jason."

"Okay, here's what happened and you'll have to forgive me for making assumptions about you but I had this feeling you wouldn't show up."

"Oh really?" I said.

"Yeah, really. I went by your work and when you weren't there, I came here. And your light was off so I called the dorm phone and no one answered. I was on my way to The Local but there's no need for that now. So where shall I take you, my dear, since you obviously don't want to go to your room?"

"Wherever you're going; I don't really care." I reached up, turned his face toward mine and kissed his lips. I laid my head against his big shoulder, thankful to be rescued from the exhausting way I grieved over Connor.

He put me down on the edge of campus. We walked along the busy little street, past Judge's, past the pizza dive where I worked, past The Local, and kept walking until we came to a side street where a charming little white house appeared vaguely familiar. "I bet you don't remember my house do you?" Jason said as we approached.

"Only leaving it," I replied.

"Well, I'm sure we can do better than that," Jason said as we walked past an old model Mercedes Benz in the driveway, up the steps to the porch, past the swing, and into the house. I hadn't noticed before but his house was beautifully furnished. There were computers all around; desktops, laptops, and monitors. It was like technology overload. "Excuse all the mess everywhere. I don't usually have visitors over, well, visitors that I'm trying to impress anyway."

"Your house is beautiful. Did you decorate and clean by yourself or does someone do that for you?"

"What? I do my own thing, babe. This is all one hundred percent Jason Hamilton Watts."

"Well, you're doing a mighty fine job, Mr. Watts," I replied.

Jason offered a beer and I accepted. He sat down on the couch and patted the seat beside him indicating for me to sit down. So I did. "I'm going to show you what I've created," he said picking up a console and turning on the TV with the remote. A video game with lifelike graphics and animation exploded onto the screen. It was some sort of war or conflict. I wasn't sure but it looked amazingly real.

"How did you do this?" I asked.

"Years of practice and lots of great professors and people leading the way. I've been really lucky," he said watching the screen and moving sticks and pressing buttons on the console. After a few seconds passed, he put the little control box down. "I hope you don't think I'm going to play video games when I have you sitting beside me," he said rubbing his hand over the top of my thigh pushing my sundress higher and higher.

"I was beginning to wonder," I said teasing him and pushing my dress back down. I got up, walked into the kitchen, brought two more beers to the couch and gave one to Jason. We drank them quickly then he grabbed me and pulled me onto his lap. We kissed while his hand finished what it had started a few minutes ago.

He carried me to his bedroom and gently placed me on the bed. His clothes came off and I saw his big beautiful body in full view before he covered me with it. Yes, Jason Watts was going to be a very effective distraction, at least for a little while.

CHAPTER 26

Fall break finally arrived and I needed some time to recover from all the studying, all the waitressing, all the distraction. But Jason wasn't having it. "Nope. There is no way you are going away for a week without me. I am driving you to Blackrock and that's that," he said in strong protest to my idea of renting a car and driving to the mountains by myself to visit Mary and Tory. It wasn't a hard sell. We packed his four-door 1970's Mercedes sedan with our bags and headed west. "I just had to get this car. I had the motor rebuilt and it's a beast. You'll see. Plus it's big enough for my long-ass legs," Jason said pulling out of the driveway.

"It's black with red leather seats. What's not to love? It's beautiful," I responded.

"I know right. This is my baby...well, my other baby," he said looking over at me with a worried, apologetic smile. I just shook my head and a little chuckle, sounding and feeling like happiness, broke through. I was really going to try to give Jason a shot at mending my broken heart.

"Maybe, just maybe," I thought to myself, "I could at least try to envision a future without Connor in it." Well, I did at least try.

Mary and Tory ran out of the front door of the bakery with

open arms when we pulled up. I hardly recognized them. It was like they had been "de-gothic-ized." Tory's infectious laughter just about put us all in hysterics before we even spoke a word.

"This is Jason." I finally said. I received two looks of worried approval. I knew why they were worried and why they approved; I was still a broken girl over Connor but a big gorgeous smiling man was standing by my side with his arm around me. He received lots of love and welcome from my sister and her best friend.

We arrived just as they were closing the bakery so we went in and sampled some of the leftover delights. "Wow, these are amazing. I'm so impressed," I said. "Oh, and I think Jason likes them too," I continued while pointing to his stuffed mouth and icing smeared face. He nodded with approval while licking his long fingers.

We headed to Mary and Tory's little wooden house nestled in a stand of trees. It was like the mountains had lifted the gothic veil to reveal two nature girls. It worked for them. We sat on their front porch and drank beers while enjoying the delicious feast they had prepared for us; salad, vegetable lasagna, garlic bread, and of course, a very special dessert. It was a cake with two thick, black layers flavored with black cherry surrounded with dark chocolate buttercream spiced with red pepper and cinnamon. "We call this our *We've Gothic So Good* cake. It's going to be our featured item when we open our own shop," Tory said.

"It has quite a kick, but it's irresistible. I need another big slice and two more tall cold ones," Jason said. He won them over with ease.

We sat on their front porch talking about the future while candles burned down to waxy puddles. Mary and Tory told us about a little space they wanted to buy and remodel for their own bakery. They told us about all the interesting names they planned to assign to their goodies such as Boys Don't Cry Cupcakes, Close to Me Muffins, Just Like Heavenly Hash Bars, Bauhaus Bon Bons. Well, the gothic hadn't completely left these girls. It was a creative and perfect idea for them.

Mary asked Jason about his plans for the future in addition to every other question in the book. His most immediate plan was to finish grad school. Then he told them what he had already told me; "I'm moving to Seattle in June. I have a pretty big job offer so I can't really turn it down." Three pairs of eyes slowly, eventually turned to me.

I thought they were gauging my reaction to Jason's plans so I bailed, "How about another round of beers?" I jumped up and scurried into the house, used the bathroom and gathered the beers. By the time I returned to the porch, the conversation had turned to what we would be doing for the next four days in the mountains of Blackrock: hiking, biking, baking, drinking, eating. I felt something similar to happiness but I could not help thinking how I wished it was Connor sitting in that chair across from me. My thoughts made me feel guilty so I tried to be that other girl; the girl who let Jason in, the girl who didn't care anymore. Beer helped so I drank down my fifth one and smiled without thinking too much about anything.

I woke up on our third morning in the mountains beside Jason, sprawled out in all his naked glory. I covered him with the sheet, slipped out of the bed, into my robe, and out of the room to the kitchen where I smelled coffee and muffins. Instead of a good morning greeting, I received two serious faces. "We need to talk, Lucy...now while Jason is still sleeping," Mary began.

"What is it?" I said a little worried by her serious tone.

She just blurted it out, "Jason is going to ask you to go to Seattle with him. He really likes you."

Tory reiterated, "...really, really likes you."

Mary continued in a hushed voice, "He told us last night. Now I want you to be honest with him and with yourself. You just need to be prepared. Don't break this man's heart, Lucy. He is good for you."

I sat there thinking; feeling blindsided. I knew he was leaving at the end of the school year and I guess I was sort of relieved about it; he would leave and I could get back to my full-time job of preparing for Connor to come back to me. I had to be ready when that happened. I couldn't be living in Seattle with some other man. "Are you crazy? I can't go to Seattle," I whispered with a little too much angst.

Mary and Tory looked at each other and nodded like they had anticipated that reply. Mary continued, "I knew it; you're not over him yet. He is married to some bimbo bitch and you are still not over him. What the hell, Lucy? Move on already."

"Listen to her, Lucy. Don't let Jason get away," Tory said backing up her best friend.

I was in shock. I was floored that these two girls were telling me to forget Connor, to go on with my life without hope of being his wife and to make a commitment to another man. These two girls, who had been there from the very beginning and knew how perfect Connor and Lucy were together, were ready, just like that, to close the door on our love affair...

"Unbelievable," I said.

"Don't break Jason's heart," Mary said.

"And don't lead him on," added Tory.

"Wow. Can I just eat my muffin now?" I said, sufficiently scolded and informed.

"Yes. So, anyway, how is Jason in bed?" Tory whispered changing the subject.

Again, I said, "Unbelievable."

Our little break from school came to an end early on the fourth morning. We packed the big Mercedes with our bags and Mary and Tory packed the back seat with enough boxes of gothic goodies to last a month. Jason hugged each one of them like they were already old friends. I got the remember-what-we-said look with my hugs. I slipped to the middle seat and held Jason's arm for most of the trip home. This was nice but I didn't feel like it was my fate. I believed in something bigger than nice, I believed in Connor and Lucy. Yes, I had messed up and let Connor go for a moment, but he had to forgive me and come back. Even with the attention I was getting from Jason, my heart refused to budge. I prayed for change, for release from this spell, but I never stopped dreaming of Connor; I never stopped crying for him. I've never stopped waiting for him to come back.

I knew that I had to tell Jason, eventually. It was wrong of me to lead him on knowing that I had never dreamed of him or envisioned my future with him in it. He had become my boyfriend, I guess, but we never talked about it. We spent a lot of time together over the months leading up to his departure and he proved to be an amazing distraction. Jason had spared me many nights of crying to exhaustion over Connor and if for no other reason, I loved him for that.

"So, I'm leaving in two months you know," Jason said finally bringing up the topic while still on top of me in his bed.

"Yeah, I know. Time has really been flying by," I replied. I braced for what was coming.

"I want you to come with me," he said stalling my answer with little kisses on my lips. "I mean, I really want you to come with me, Lucy. I've thought a lot about it and I'm sure."

No more stalling; I had to tell him now. I struggled from underneath his big body and began, "You remember at the coffee shop when you said I could tell you whatever it was that I needed to shake and that you were a really good listener. Well, I think I need to take you up on that tonight."

We sat across from each other in his bed while I told him my story of Connor and Lucy. I began with how we met on Judd Street. Then I told him how Connor loved my family despite our many flaws and how he took me to meet his family and his grandparents. I told him about the letters he wrote to me from the desert when he was sent to war, and how he had asked me to marry him when he returned. I told him how it had scared the hell out of me and that I let him go long enough to mess up only to realize that I wanted nothing more than to be with him. I told Jason how Connor left me standing on the corner lot and never looked back and that he was married now.

"I wish I could let go of him but I can't. I wanted you to be the one to fix me...to change me...but I know I'm still waiting for him. I'm sorry, Jason. You are an amazing lover and boyfriend, if that's what you've been to me. It's not fair to you for me to pretend like I'm not in love with someone else though. I can't go to Seattle with you."

Jason's silence was devastating to me. "Do you want me to leave?" I asked, thinking he was either furious or heart-broken...or both.

"No, I don't want you to go," he said taking my hand in his. He reached over, placed a finger under my chin, gently lifted my hanging head, and pleaded his case. "Lucy, he's married. Can't you even consider the possibility that maybe he's not who you thought he was? I mean, so soon after you broke up he's found some other girl to replace you just like that...and then married her. Come on. You're smarter than that. You can grow from it, learn from it. I'm here, right here, choosing you while he's...God only knows. Lucy, wake up for God's sake."

Jason was getting upset. He let go of my hand and got off the bed. It was silent as he headed for the bathroom except for that pushy bitch in my head screaming, "He is absolutely right. Jason is great. Don't do this. Don't let him go. You'll never find someone like him again. Be happy! Go with Jason!!!" But she obviously had no connection to my heart because it was guiding me down only one path: Connor Hawthorn. What a stubborn, stubborn heart I possess.

Jason came out of the bathroom after several minutes with an easier, more relaxed demeanor. He climbed back in bed beside me and said, "You and I had an agreement up front, didn't we? I remember; I was going to be a distraction. It's not your fault that I took it further. I think you're setting yourself up to be hurt by this guy again. I care about you and I want you to find a way to get over him."

"Thank you. I have been trying. I'm just not ready to give up yet," I said.

"Okay then, I have just one question for you. Since the truth is out and I know where I stand, can I continue distracting you until I leave?" I looked at him relieved that there wasn't going to be a scene, no breakdown or outrage.

"Yes...please. And thank you for being so wonderful to me."
We kissed passionately as he did some of his best distracting.
Then we slept in each other's arms in the cool darkness of his
bedroom until life forced us out into a new day.

****

I felt horrible. Hurting Jason was not my intention but what
did I expect? I gave myself over to him in every way except the
only way that mattered: he got all of me except for my heart.
That wasn't fair. I tried to stay away from him during those last
few weeks by over burdening myself with work, class, study,
and I even took up jogging to release suppressed emotions and
as a means to clear my head. It was no use though...I always
ended up at Jason's.

We packed his belongings and shipped them to Seattle. We
sold his beautiful furniture. He ended his lease on the quaint
little house. Jason was gone too soon. On his last day, he drove
me across campus in his big black Mercedes to drop me off on his
way out of town. He was about to begin his big road trip, driving
all the way across the country to begin his new life. I was painfully aware that I could have been beside him the entire way.
But no; I chose to stay the course, to follow my heart, to wait for
my true love to come back because I knew he would.

Our hug was long by anyone's standards. I cried because I
missed him already. He didn't cry; he was just ready to leave and
who could blame him? I kissed him one last time on his big, soft
lips. He put his rattling diesel engine in reverse and backed out
of my life. That could have been the life I was meant to have.
But I let it go and did not look back. I walked up the stairs to
my dorm room and was thankful that Ashley had moved. She
wasn't there to confirm the fact that I was a complete idiot for

not sitting in the middle seat holding on to Jason's arm all the way to Seattle. I felt regretful about not going with him, but he just wasn't Connor; that was his only flaw.

If not Connor, if not Henry, if not Jason, then who? Maybe I was destined to be alone. It was my nature after all. One word kept creeping up when I thought about my future. The only word that could describe what I needed was "drastic." I needed drastic change, circumstances, and challenges beyond anything I had ever experienced. I needed to go far away, drastically far... Timbuktu far. Africa actually seemed far enough so I began the arduous task of applying for the Peace Corps. I had to keep trying to shed the old Lucy because she was too sad, too broken, too forgotten. Lucy would never have the nerve to go to Africa. The application process took a lot of effort and an entire year. I finally received my assignment: Teacher - Benin, West Africa.

Who was I kidding? I couldn't completely forget Lucy as much as I wanted to. After graduation, even with Africa on my horizon, one thing, and one thing only, was on my mind.

CHAPTER 27

****

Is time enough to make you see
I never meant to set you free
And now you know not who I am
A stranger in a foreign land
Without you, see, I don't know me
A stranger I will always be.

It's funny how we are programmed for self-preservation. My mind was starting to shift; probably some biological, evolutionary tactic to keep me from completely succumbing to my burdensome disappointment. I began to think of benign things like how the cement bench was surprisingly cool in the shade considering the humid Georgia heat, and how I couldn't wait to eat since my stomach had been unable to handle any breakfast and it was, at this point, way past lunch. I was sitting there near the commons area on his college campus waiting to get my Connor back when it hit me, he's not coming.

I was at a pivotal crossroads in my life. If I saw his green eyes and he saw mine, I was sure without a doubt that he would unearth the love he had buried for me just a few short years ago. I could actually feel him ease into the space beside me and take my hand squeezing my fingertips between his fingers like he had done so many times before. So powerful is suggestion and desire that I could feel pressure as though my hand was being held and for a moment I closed my eyes, imagining him right there. I opened them when the reality of my four-hour long wait shook me kind of like a rescuer grabbing both of my shoulders and shaking me to regain consciousness, "HE'S NOT COMING!"

If he didn't show, I would have no excuse now not to go. In two weeks I would be on my way to Africa for two years to serve out my term as a Peace Corps volunteer. My deepest secret desire which prompted my five-hour drive from North Carolina to Savannah the previous night was that we would meet and see each other as we had during the first days of our relationship, just like the night I found him in the kitchen on Judd Street, and fall in love all over again. I wished we could pick up where we had fallen apart and I would forego the trip to Africa altogether since my fear for this escape from reality was so thick that I could practically hold it in my hands. If given a choice this time, I would choose Georgia, marriage, babies, anything as long as I was with Connor.

My plan was to arrive in Savannah, call him from my motel room, and lie; something I was still unable to do with any amount of skill. I would tell him that one of my girlfriends had made the trip to visit a childhood friend and didn't want to drive all the way by herself; a reasonable excuse for showing up there. I checked in at the Holiday Inn around 8:00pm. I caught an unfortunate glimpse of myself in the oversized mirror leading into the bathroom. For just a moment, I stared into my own eyes thinking about what led me to this room reaching so desperately for something, most likely, already gone. I remembered Mary and Tory's advice in the mountains, and I recalled Jason's big Mercedes driving away from me, my empty seat beside him. The only word that crept up was "pathetic."

So I hesitantly dialed his number (Trudi had written it as a P.S. on a reply to some random card I sent her last year. I believe she was also still hoping). My eyes were closed, my hands were trembling, and my head was already shaking with regret while his phone rang once...twice...three times. Tears welled deep and then quickly rolled down my face when I heard his voice.

"Hello." I was proceeding, in spite of myself, without caution.

"Hi. May I speak to Connor?" The pulsing silence seemed to last unreasonably long.

"Is this Lucy?" He recognized my voice.

"Yeah, yes it is. How are you?"

"I'm fine. How are you? This is such a surprise."

"I'm great. I'm actually in Savannah until tomorrow night. I came to keep my friend company. She's meeting an old friend and she didn't want to make the trip alone. I was hoping we could meet somewhere and have a cup of coffee or something."

"Um, yeah, I don't know, wow. I'm in shock to hear from you right now. I actually have a class in the morning but I'm done by 12:30. I guess we could meet then, after my class in the commons area." This was going as planned and not so pathetic after all.

"That sounds great. I can't wait to see you," I said trying to keep my cool.

"Yeah, me too. So I'll see you tomorrow then, after my class."

My lie had actually, seemingly worked. I was about to reconnect with my long lost love. I wondered if my going to get him counted as him coming back to me. Maybe I was toying too much with fate, you know, forcing it. This wasn't exactly him coming back to me after years of being set free. But I couldn't bring myself to care. I was going to see Connor Hawthorn tomorrow. It had almost been five years. I slept soundly, too hopeful, on the edge of my fairytale.

There is one detail I am undermining, an annoyance really. Connor had married again. This was his second marriage since our breakup and I could not bring myself to take it seriously. I knew that he was still in love with me; at least that was *my* reality.

Trudi reassuringly wrote to me, *"Connor is just running, baby. God only knows from what. I guess he's just lost right now and honestly believes that getting married and starting a family is where he'll find happiness, or himself, or whatever it is he's looking for. Go ahead and live your life. Don't wait on him. If it's meant to be, then it will be."*

This was her commentary on her son's *ridiculous phase*. She didn't understand why I couldn't let go and move on with my life. As a matter of fact, I couldn't understand it either. All I knew for sure was that my heart still belonged to her son and nothing had been able to change that.

My trip to Georgia was just a desperate attempt to get back what I felt was rightfully mine: my happily ever after with Connor. If this turned out badly, I would be on my way to Africa, a world away from him for a destructive amount of time. I, like Connor, was planning to run. I, too, was searching and lost. There at my crossroads, on a strangely cool cement bench on his college campus, Connor chose my direction for me. He let me go again. It felt like I was falling into space, a hollow, imploding, lifeless planet: spinning head, racing heart, sadness like gravity holding me down on the bench and seeping out of my pores. He's not coming.

At 4:30pm I broke out of my trance, grabbed my purse, and walked to the payphone inside the student union. I inserted my coin and dialed his number, again proceeding without caution in spite of myself. He answered the phone with a deadpan voice as if he knew the call would be a stressful one, "Hello?"

"Connor, you didn't come. I've been waiting."

"Oh my God, are you still there? I thought you would have been gone by now."

"Why, I mean...what happened? Is everything ok?"

Now, for the truth. "I just can't see you, Lucy. You know it's more than just coffee. I'm married and I'm really trying to do the right thing here."

My disappointment and shock finally took over, "I came all the way here to see you. I LIED about my friend. I'm here by myself. I just need to see you before I leave for Africa. I need to know for sure."

"You shouldn't have come all the way here, Lucy. And why are you going to Africa of all places? No, never mind. Don't tell me."

"Are you sure you can't just come meet me for like ten minutes. I need this, Connor."

With a detectable amount of strain in his voice, his final message cracked, "No. I have to go now, Lucy. I'm so sorry." And just like that, the phone call ended.

I hung up the receiver and stood there collecting myself for a minute, then calmly walked to my rental car, got in, and methodically drove. It's funny how little I remember about my hopeful drive to Savannah the day before but my trip home is etched in my memory. As I left the city limits and looked back through the rearview mirror, imagining some other woman coming home to my dream, my composure crumbled. I drove through a shower of grief, tears, loud crying, silent sobbing, gripping the steering wheel, pounding it with my fist. It hurt worse this time. It felt like the end. There was no "if it comes back" for me. I reached the point that night in my rental car when I could no longer cry.

Then, swithcing into survivor-mode and feeling completely numb, I set my sights on Africa. With Connor an unreachable, faded reality once more, I was ready to run, to get lost, to disappear. All of a sudden, the other side of the ocean was just what I needed...drastically. The next chapter of my life without Connor was about to begin.

I stayed at my parents' trailer for three days before I had to leave for Washington D.C. for volunteer orientation, but before I left, I had to shred them all. I had to destroy the words that mocked me now more than ever. For two days I sat in the room by my ailing dad with my mom's light load shredder, reading and then numbly sending each page of each letter through, occasionally smiling at his little boy handwriting: *"Just trying this on, Mrs. Lucy Hawthorn. I like that."* I loved those letters too much, and their existence was killing me. It seemed only fitting for these words written by him to meet their violent end at the churning of metal blades, pushed through by the forgotten hands he used to dream of holding. I couldn't bear to read one more word on any of those sheets of stationary I had cherished for so many years since receiving them when he was in Saudi Arabia.

The words Connor had written to me were just not true anymore. I felt the magic slipping – "if it comes back, then it was really yours." I guess the "if" decided against us.

I shredded those letters that had been carefully stored in three shoe boxes in my tiny closet. I shredded his thoughts written down daily while he was a soldier at war, desperately missing me. I might have just shredded my heart in that little machine but for some reason, a flicker of hope remained. I mean we were meant to be, no matter what Connor thought or who he married. Though my letters were destroyed, my heart was still sort of beating, and it still, unquestionably, belonged to him. So I held my dad's cold, fragile hand, placed my forehead down on it, and told him goodbye, aware that he was near the end. Then I buried myself under blankets on my parents' couch and waited until I had to come out; until it was time to run away from everything I had ever known in search of something drastically new.

CHAPTER 28

****

Memories linger on and on,
Never leaving me alone
Teasing life with joyous lies,
And watching as the fire dies
One spark in me left to light,
My candle burns alone tonight.

Maybe there are golden threads connecting us to the people who are supposed to be in our lives. If so, when the tension is the same on both ends there is harmony. If the threads are being tugged harder on one end than on the other, there is heartache. I had no choice but to pretend I had loosened my steely grip on the thread that held me so firmly attached to Connor after returning home from my failed trip to Georgia. Things should have been balanced between us as it seemed Connor had certainly let go of our particular golden thread. But now, all of a sudden, the tugging was coming from the other end.

While my family and I stood in the hotel parking lot in Washington, D.C. hugging, saying our goodbyes, and holding onto our golden threads, Mom's phone was ringing in North Carolina.

Connor's voice filled the kitchen through the answering machine and no one was there to hear it, except for my dad who was too weak to answer.

"Hi, it's Connor. I was just wondering if Lucy has already left for Africa. I wanted to apologize for being a jerk when she came to see me. If it's at all possible, please have her call me at this number..."

The van door closed and I was on my way to the airport, looking back, waving to my family, and intentionally putting an ocean of distance between us. While I had been packing for Africa, Connor had also been packing. He was leaving his second failed marriage and I was leaving the continent. Maybe this is where the magic behind the message almost worked. Was Connor trying to come back to me but the timing was all wrong? It was as if my fireflies were returning to my backyard for another sparkling performance and no one was there to see it. Had I been home and able to take that call, I wonder how my life might have changed.

****

I was sitting in a rocking chair with my arms tenderly embracing my very pregnant belly. In the pastel cloudiness, I got up from my chair and began walking toward a fading figure. I believed it was Connor in the distance. My peaceful expression changed to panic and I began running as the figure completely faded away. I was running for my life. I woke up from this nightmare, gripping my very unpregnant empty belly, out of breath and self-conscious, as the plane encountered a slight disturbance causing the "fasten your seatbelt" sign to come on with a loud ding. "Wow, Lucy, way to start your drastic new adventure," I thought to myself, annoyed at how even my subconscious was hell-bent on pining for Connor. I was sad after leaving Mom, Mary, and Tory behind; and even though my dad had been a mean old bastard, I knew he wouldn't last two more years and that I had probably seen him for the last time.

I couldn't believe that I, Lucy Bells, was actually sitting on a plane bound for Africa. I looked around at the other fifty or so new Peace Corps volunteers exchanging stories and information and becoming friends. I sat pensive and unapproachable; a derelict in the worst way. I said a quick prayer that I would allow myself to open up, have thoughts beyond this heavy introspection, stop hating myself for hurting Jason, and finally get past this first love bullshit. I needed to embrace this new drastic reality. I desperately needed to change.

After a thirteen-hour flight, I was about to feel real African heat and I was so ready. I mean, I thought I was ready until I approached the exit door. At that moment, I was taken back to my grandmother's kitchen; a little girl standing too close to the oven when she opened it to pull out the chocolate chip cookies. It was that same kind of scorching heat on my face. I thought, "Welcome to Africa, Lucy. This just might work." I descended the steps of the plane, approaching the Third World with a new, heightened survival mentality. Tending to my broken heart would have to wait for now, and with this distance between us, I thought I might even find a way to get over Connor. But I've always been wrong.

The calloused, annoyed employees at the small, heavily secured airport were not fascinated by us "Yovos," a name all white-skinned people were called in Benin. They simply made our trip through customs easy as we were Peace Corps volunteers and everything had been pre-arranged for our arrival. Nevertheless, this façade of organization did not ease the anxiety.

It was outside the front doors of the airport where the adventure really began. My senses, so spoiled by scented candles, fabric softener, and anything from Bath and Body Works were the first things to be accosted. It smelled bad, like body musk and feces. And forget the American expectation of personal space. Children would mercilessly surround us just to touch our skin and hair; all of them...all at once...all yelling and jumping up and down.

An official Peace Corps van driven by an overly-eager African man smiling with gleaming white teeth was waiting to transport us through the bustling beach-side city of Cotonou. All my preconceived notions of Africa being a sandpit with forgotten children dying of starvation with their swollen bellies and blank faces covered in flies were quickly forgotten. Beautiful blue skies stretched overhead as palm trees lined networks of paved roads. I could not believe the activity, the vibrant colors, the noises, and the carnival atmosphere. Nothing could have convinced me of this before arriving. To believe this Africa, one must see, hear, smell, and feel it.

Women and young girls carried on with life while balancing brightly painted metal basins on their heads filled with various hygiene products for sale. Children hustled any and everyone to buy soap, candy, tools, or whatever they could fit in their sacks. The fabrics wrapped around the women's and girls' bodies were brilliantly colored red, blue, yellow, and green and had unusual images on them such as radios, batteries, and toothbrushes. The men and boys just wore jeans and t-shirts or button-down shirts made from the off-beat materials that painted the dusty landscape kaleidoscope crazy. A never-ending rotation of various Afro-pop sensations filled the air, blasting from speakers in terrible need of woofers and tweeters. Little mopeds operated by men in yellow button-down shirts carrying passengers here and there jammed the streets to a virtual standstill. They did not seem to follow any rules of order or safety, in fact, neither did the vehicles. There was chaos on the streets. This city was just as alive as New York or Miami and it literally seemed to be reaching out with intent to grab us Yovos and pull us in.

I happened to sit beside a tall, lanky, blonde American male in the white van. We looked at each other with childlike amazement, not knowing each other from Adam, only finding ourselves shell-shocked in the same spot on the globe at this most insane moment. In a burst of juvenile excitement, we grabbed each other and hugged. I think we both let out a high-pitched yelp and jumped in our seats like little kids. I felt the tension drop like an anvil from my body. I thought, "I can do this. I can do this."

We soon arrived at a building that resembled a cheap, two-level motel. We filed out of the vans looking around like tourists and did what our African guides told us to do, "Find a room, a bed, and meet us here again to retrieve your bags." I was given a mosquito net and one of six bunk beds in a dorm-like setting on the second floor. Twelve of us shared the room. We selected our bunks, secured our possessions, and assembled downstairs crowding under a tree to escape the sun's direct heat. We were led into a large room where a long table was filled with food: pineapple, croissants, baguettes, rice, pasta, salad, skewered lamb, and steak. It was a surprising feast. There were Cokes in little glass bottles just like the old days back home. We were free to eat, drink, and mingle, the last of which I was ill-prepared. My van-friend and I gravitated toward each other and solidified our friendship. Brett was from Georgia, like Connor, which had an unreasonable effect on me. I wanted to be near him for that reason alone. We ate, exchanged stories, and expressed our excitement and fears.

Four Africans entered the room dressed in full cultural attire but unlike the haphazard designs worn by the street vendors, these materials were more dignified with geometrical, tribal patterns in deep earth tones. They would be our teachers over the next three months as we moved from the bustling city of Cotonou to various smaller villages for training. They would attempt to teach us how to survive in Africa. Right away, they introduced themselves in English, spoken with a unique Afro-French accent. "I am Idrissu, and I am honored to welcome you here to our country. I am joined by Renee, David, and Samuel who also wish to welcome you to Benin." We applauded and they mingled among us for more personal introductions.

At the facility we rested, adjusted, and readjusted. We spent three days there in the city of Cotonou individually tending to our delicate stomachs and assessing whether or not this was really the best idea for our lives. We had three days to get used to the food, the water, and the heat before we left the city. It was as if we were on another planet; like we had completely been transported.

My first call home came on that third day before we moved on to more remote locations. It was planned that way by the Peace Corps staff; three days, no contact with familiar voices. "Break 'em in hard" seemed to be the motto in Benin.

"He called. While you were getting on the plane, Connor called the house wanting to talk to you." Mom hoped her words would prompt me to quickly find my way back home so that I could stop running away, return that call, and get my life back with Connor. Instead, her words were like a huge hand grabbing my black construction paper heart, and effortlessly crushing it. I felt like time and opportunity had defeated me; like fate had played a ruthless joke for which I was the butt.

Out of my mind with delusions of Africa helping to mend my broken heart, I said through cracking vocals, "I'm here now and I need to try to get over him." Then, suppressing the overwhelming wave of mixed emotions welling up inside of me, I continued with more angst in my voice, "Mom, I have come all the way to Africa and I'm not leaving until I have completely rid myself of him. Please don't tell me anything more about him."

"Lucy, you have to make your own decisions and I will support you," Mom said, just trying to do the right thing.

On how many occasions, about how many things, could one person be so wrong?

CHAPTER 29

I had other things besides Connor on my mind for once as I sat on my duffle bag by a flooded river. It wasn't exactly the Nile, but the dirt road had been blocked by this deluge and the African driver thought it would be sufficient to just unload me right there: three boxes filled with provisions for survival in my most remote northern village, a bookbag on my back, and a duffle bag filled with useless clothes from home. I didn't even try to debate this with him as my French wasn't strong enough to make a good case for myself. The road was blocked. His mission to deliver me to my worksite had been accomplished as best he could, and so he felt satisfied that his job was done. My link to civilization disappeared in a thick cloud of brown dust.

I wasn't afraid. I had just spent three months in training living in a family compound with children, chickens and goats roaming free while I culturally adjusted to naked breasts everywhere. I was getting accustomed to rockstar-level fame as little kids hesitantly reached out just to touch my white skin, screamed in a shrill voice at contact, and then ran like hell. What I really wanted was some shade. Never having been so close to the equator before, I could deeply feel my new proximity to the sun. I used to think nothing could be more miserable than a hot, humid summer day in North Carolina but I was wrong. This new latitude was torture on my fair skin. It was burning hot, I mean burning. I wished someone had suggested I bring an umbrella instead of seven ankle-length stretchy cotton dresses that would all soon be traded out for a couple of pieces of material to wrap around my body. It wasn't so much "When in Rome, do as the Romans do," as it was "When in Africa...survive."

But I was stranded by this river in this foreign land, feeling deserted by the driver of the air-conditioned SUV. I watched as the dust cloud settled like the portal to my old world closing and disappearing, leaving me here in this new world at the complete mercy of the natives. His assumption that I had been adequately prepared to fend for myself was just wrong. So I did what I do best; I observed.

African women bent completely over at the waist made no waste of the floodwater as they lined up to wash their colorful cotton wraps (called "panyas"), polyester slips, bloomers, and whatever other Western goodwill rejects they owned. These items covered the immediate shore like a patchwork quilt lying right out on the sandy ground to dry. The children in their dirty, puffy drawers splashed in the shallows near their mothers.

The men perplexed me the most. They seemed occupied but not really intent on anything in particular. They certainly weren't lifting a finger to help with the laundry or the children. Some sat in little bits of shade provided by the trunks of lifeless trees that appeared mangled and bleached white by the sun; some of them brandishing thorns as long as my middle finger. These trees seemed like something that would have grown in Dante's version of Hell. Other men talked ceaselessly and all at the same time while their arms were flying about. I wondered how in the world each knew what the other had said.

Eventually, a homemade canoe that looked like a glorified strip of warped wood came as if by the workings of God. It was manned by a scoundrel who happily took my money as a fee to get across the river. My belongings were loaded first and then I entered the rickety vessel thinking, "Oh well, here goes nothing." I speculated that the men had devised this plan as a money-making venture with all their theatrics. I really didn't care at that point because even in my role as the helpless American, I was, once again, on the move.

Unfortunately, my progress was short-lived. The waiting game commenced yet again on the other bank of the flooded river while another African with a car was commissioned to drive me to my village on the Niger River, Bello Tounga, or "Beautiful Village" in translation. The car arrived and could have been lumped in the same lemon category as the canoe: a rusty hull with wheels that would have never passed state inspection in North Carolina. My belongings were tossed in a dirty trunk and I was hustled into the backseat followed by three other adult Africans that I did not even realize were also waiting for transportation. I was thinking how unsafe this arrangement was. Were there any emergency personnel within a day's travel from here? Where were the seatbelts? The joke was always on me. I paid my fare and after four more Africans piled in the front seat beside the driver, the nine of us were on our way.

The driver tore from the flooded river bank and seemed to be turning that enormous wheel freely as the car swayed back and forth, catching air over the hills and dips in the red dirt road.

My communication with the driver was basic, "Bello Tounga!" It seemed that we had been on the verge of actual flight down a straight and narrow dirt road for the extent of my entire life (my concept of time was already skewing) with vast emptiness on either side. To say that I wanted this trip to end would be a severe understatement.

Finally, amid endless, incomprehensible conversation in the front seat, I began to hear tokens of familiarity sounding like, "Yayayadohhehayayaho Bello Tounga!!!! Yayaya." And something similar would spill from another's mouth in reply. If we were heading due north, the sudden, sharp right turn we took would have changed our course directly east, but I had no idea about direction as my inner compass was completely shot. Anyway, I assumed we were now heading toward Bello Tounga, my home for the next two years.

Along the route, I saw a soccer field with genuine goals at both ends. I also saw a brick building with an A-line rooftop and wooden doors. Both of these oddities were sticking out from the barren landscape like props from a movie set long abandoned. It appeared that Bello Tounga had already been touched by the Western world. "How can I top a soccer field?" I thought. We were headed straight for the village now and ironically, I wished for more road.

On the final approach, a welcoming committee showed up. Children, running dangerously close to the speeding vehicle, were screaming and hitting the car with their outstretched hands. I could not tell the gender of individuals and only assumed the ones wearing loose-fitting, worn-thin and faded cotton dresses were girls. They announced my arrival at Bello Tounga.

The car came to a sudden halt at the edge of the world. What a quaint and tidy village I had been assigned. Everything was made from the earth and had already been sustainable for hundreds of years. What was I doing here? I had to remember to keep focused and never stop working. The Peace Corps slogan was ringing in my head, "The toughest job you'll ever love." This wasn't supposed to be easy.

I was still just an oddity, a new toy of sorts, a point of interest. But life had to go on and so the spectacle of my arrival was short-lived. They had things to do before the sunset and they *had* to get them done; a concept I would come to understand very soon.

My belongings were carried to my new home by over-eager boys and girls, smiling from ear-to-ear. It was easy to tell which hut was meant for me because, compared to the others, it was quite nice. A big cement patio had been laid out in front of the hut designated for me and it was surrounded by a privacy fence made of straw; though bent and leaning over so much that I had a perfect view of the entire façade. This hut was on one end connected to four other family huts. There were huts built all around. I was surrounded by huts; all of them serving five to ten people. Mine served only one. The different sized rocks and pieces of straw that were mixed in before the mud solidified made the little dwellings look like extensions of the land.

A few pieces of furniture supplied by the Peace Corps were already waiting for me: single mattress, wooden bed frame, bookshelf, small table. Every volunteer was issued a double-burner gas stove and a tank of butane. Americans could not survive on Africa's untreated water so I would be boiling all of the water I consumed. They also gave me a mosquito net which, coupled with the little pink pill I had to take every day, would keep me safe from the fevers of malaria. These items kept me alive while I was in Africa. Without them, I might have lived a few months.

I relieved myself by squatting over a deep hole in the ground that had been fortified with a cheap dome of cement by the Peace Corps and surrounded by a straw fence. But that was better than what my fellow villagers had; they went right in the tall grass surrounding the village. I would take my bucket baths standing on another slab of cheap cement behind another straw fence. Both of these utilities were right outside the back door of my hut. All in all, it was a very convenient and privileged residence in Bello Tounga.

"Ver-on-ica!, Ver-on-ica! Ver-on-ica!" Were they actually calling *me* Ver-on-ica or just lamenting that I wasn't Ver-on-ica? I never knew how defensive over my name and identity I could be until I had neither of my own. The volunteer who had been assigned here before me was named Veronica and boy, did the villagers ever let me know it. I felt lame and insufficient because before she left, she had completely integrated herself into their lives by speaking their language fluently and choosing to eat their food. I arrived incapable of doing either. As they spoke, all I could understand were the frequent interjections of the name "Ver-on-ica" and the disapproving glances toward me that followed.

All I needed was a little time and Africa offered it up in slow, lingering hours. Firstly, they must learn my name: "Luuu-ceeee," I would say. "Luuu-theeeeee," they would attempt with a strong lisp and then scowl. No one liked it so they called me "Hassia." Deezay, the matron of the village, decided this and so it was as good as law. I had no choice, no say in the matter. I was called Hassia for the extent of my stay in their village. My identity was quickly being ripped away from me like a security blanket being taken from a child. I knew this was no place for the weak at heart and so I had to toughen up.

CHAPTER 30

I don't remember my first night in Bello Tounga but I'm sure it was like the many that followed. Nights were a time of peace and quiet except for the crackling and popping of the wood in small fires set throughout the village to ward off flies and mosquitoes. Low mumblings of an ancient tribal language added a layer of soothing comfort, like a distant lullaby pulsing through the darkness. As the moon phased out of sight each month, more stars than I could have imagined fitting in the sky burst into view with the setting sun. Constellations stuck out like sore thumbs in the surrounding pitch dark. I lay on my back and outlined them with my finger remembering that time in the mountains...foiling my efforts to get over Connor.

Before I could rest my head, if torrential rains were not falling, I had to bring my mattress outside to the cement slab since it was too stifling to sleep inside the hut. Then I had to tie up the mosquito net to four fence posts, collect my kerosene lamp, journal and pencil. Now I could slip into my little private world and be alone. Too often it was spent thinking about what might have been with Connor and me, or filing through daily operational necessities, or drifting through deep philosophical black holes: "What is my purpose in life? How the hell could any place be so hot? Should I have gone home in response to Connor's call? How can these tiny mosquitoes make that much noise? Do I have enough water boiled for tomorrow? What will these children ever know of the world beyond the reaches of this inhospitable place? 'Location, location, location' is really the foundation of everything on earth." Sleep was a welcomed escape from my spinning mind. I dreamed of sweet things like cupcakes with buttercream icing, mint chocolate chip ice cream, Capt'n Crunch in chocolate milk, Diet Pepsit with crushed ice...Taco Bell.

I woke up each morning before dawn to the "swish, swish, swish" of straw brooms sweeping away a thin layer of dirt and dust that had settled on the ground overnight. Once it was all swept away, the hard ground emerged, and then the morning sun burned its direct heat on Bello Tounga with a vengeance.

There was a lack of urgency in Africa where politeness took precedence over punctuality, like time was standing still. The culture was rich and thick like a hot stew and I had to learn it, live it, and like it for two years.

My first days in the village were spent building a cultural bridge. A big part of that bridge was learning how to communicate...how to speak the native language, Dendi. Understanding how to greet someone in Dendi was an essential and monumental task. Greetings were a way of life.

The greeting begins when a person says, "Fo Fo" (HI!!)

In response, you would repeat, "Fo Fo!!"

Then you would be asked an array of questions, "Meta ga?" (How is your body?) "Meta foo?" (How is your home?) and so on and on and on...

And after each one of the inquiries, you would be expected to exclaim, "Bani samii" (Great!!) over and over – even if it was a lie and you were at your wit's end.

Every day, numerous times, I was asked how everything was from my body to my food, to my home, children, parents, prayer, work, etc. These salutations could go on for three or four minutes with every elder I encountered. In contrast to my culture, these lengthy ramblings were a roadblock in the way of progress. I wanted to just say "hi" and keep it moving, but Bello Tounga taught me how life was lived closer to the sun: slow-paced polite survival.

Sandy roads were another factor slowing down my American work ethic. Often times I would have to ride my bike to the next village for a women's group meeting to promote the inclusion of soybeans in their diets or for a meeting with government liaisons about building a new school. That would take about two hours of slow pedaling. Then, after no one showed up for the meeting, there would be a two-hour bike ride back to Bello Tounga through those sandy dirt roads, greeting the same village elders again with the same repetitious chorus of "Fo Fo. Metta ga? Metta foo? Metta quinyay?" I'm thinking, "Didn't I just go through this with you?" The last one, "Metta quinyay," was just silly, "How is your husband?" Of course, everything, even my imaginary husband, was "BANI SAMII!"

After mastering the time-consuming Dendi salutations, the children of Bello Tounga taught me more of their language during walks around the village. I would point to an object, they would tell me what it was in their language, and I would write it down in my notebook phonetically beside its English term. A particular phrase caught my ear because it was repeated after almost everything that was said: "Da Iquay baa!" I figured out over time that it meant, "If it is the Will of God," which just provided more philosophical mind-spinning under the stars.

These lessons were the highlight of many endless days spent in Bello Tounga. The children, so hungry and dirty, literally running around with swollen bellies, cuts and scrapes caked with dirt and flies, were thrilled beyond reason just to be with me. Past all that distraction were their eyes, their individual personalities and souls. I came to know and love a few of those dirty, smiling, scarred faces that had been cut purposefully by their parents at birth. They believed in scarring their children before life did; a telling reality of life in the raw. Bello Tounga, a beautiful village indeed.

CHAPTER 31

My job as a teacher began about a month after I arrived in Bello Tounga. In this remote village, I was supposed to focus mostly on teaching French, since formal education was a relatively new concept this far away from civilization. I drew a large square under a baobab tree and within its borders was my classroom. Five excited children and I swept the ground for an hour before the sun came up.

Children of all ages were invited to attend as long as they at least came up to my waist and were younger than marrying age as determined by their parents. The smallest children sat in the first rows and the tallest sat in the back. There were no desks so they sat right on the clean, hard ground. I began on the first day by greeting my thirty-seven students in French, "Bonjour, tout le monde." Their foreheads wrinkled above perplexed expressions. I simply repeated it several times as I walked among them in their tidy rows and held out my hand for a proper handshake. Soon, they were mimicking what I had done; attempting to speak the French greeting and shaking hands with those seated near. Other lessons were taught in the same way, listen and repeat.

I realized my progress would be small compared to teachers in the less rural areas of Benin. My students had to work just to survive: scavenge, repair living quarters, fish in the river, tend to the village livestock, fetch water from the well, collect wood for fires, etc. These things had to get done whether or not they learned how to count or greet in French. I set my school hours from seven to ten each morning. It was the highlight of their day - and mine. They showed up, smiling and willing to learn.

Before I set up my mosquito net most nights, five of my students, one boy and four girls, showed up on my cement patio for a little tutoring. They taught me more about their language while I helped them with French. Over time, I came to know and care about these kids in particular. These students might have been sixth or seventh graders in the US but I had no way of knowing how old they really were since they did not keep a conventional calendar or keep track of birthdays.

The only real milestone that mattered was when girls started their menstrual cycles. This meant that they were ready for marriage. I lost several of my students because of this. They were married off to other families in exchange for a cow, a few goats, or sometimes money. These girls had to leave Bello Tounga and live in another village. It was scary for them and it made me deeply sad to see them leave. I was especially sad when I lost one of the girls from our nighttime tutoring group to this fate. I saw the fear and pain behind their fake smiles. They were, by my culture's standards, too young to be married; too young to leave their families and friends. But I was far from my culture in almost every way.

One universal truth revealed itself during those tutoring sessions on my cement patio; a truth that surpassed cultural barriers. I realized that teenagers will be teenagers whether they are from the most rural African village or Beverly Hills.

Hassaria and Amedu liked each other and would have been boyfriend and girlfriend if they knew of such a concept. They always sat beside each other on my patio, poking fun at each other, all the while giggling and flirting. Hassaria's younger sisters, Zoowayla and Zoowayba, would gossip about the couple and try to embarrass them by parading around holding hands and fluttering their eyes at each other. Hassaria and Amedu would protest loudly followed by, "Da Iquay baa!!"

Everything was by the will of God, even when Hassaria started her period and was immediately betrothed to a boy she had never met in a village miles and miles away from Bello Tounga. One evening, after Amedu found out what was happening, he disappeared and was gone for three days. It was obvious that he was hurt and angry. Upon his return to the village, he acted out by fighting with other village boys, neglecting his chores, and even quit coming to school. It didn't take long before his actions caused him to suffer severe beatings by the hands of his father and older brothers while Hassaria and other villagers looked on. Hassaria cried hysterically and then suffered her own beating by the hands of her father and older brothers for publicly showing emotion for a boy.

Rabee, who I believed to be the youngest of my nighttime tutoring friends, stood by me during the dramatic theatrics, trembling with fear. I wondered if she imagined this happening to her someday soon. I wrapped my arm around her and repeated a couple of times, "Da Iquay baa, Rabee." This seemed to be the final analysis of everything in Bello Tounga.

Hassaria left late one evening when a small group of men showed up with her dowry, a bull that would be used for labor and eventually for meat. She left with nothing in her hands, only the materials she had wrapped around her body and over her head. Strangers led her away from the only village she had ever known, from her mother and father, brothers and sisters, Amedu, and school. She was going to live with strangers, to be a stranger's wife, to have children with him, to work hard for the rest of her days. My heart broke for her, for Amedu, and for all the children of Bello Tounga whose hearts would lead them to the ones they loved, but whose culture would steer them away.

CHAPTER 32

Six months in Bello Tounga seemed like I had already spent a lifetime away from running water, real food, and air conditioning. After Hassaria left, I had to take a break from the "Beautiful Village" in exchange for a little civilization. I arranged with one of the village elders for a taxi to arrive within the next week to pick me up. Three days later, the same old car that delivered me to Bello Tounga arrived to help me escape back to Cotonou. I packed my bookbag with a few changes of clothes and bid farewell to my village family and a few of my students who had gathered along the dirt road. I jumped into the back seat of that car, not even remotely concerned about its state of disrepair, and held on tight as the driver floored the gas pedal. He turned that big steering wheel left and right and caught air over the hills and dips in the endless stretch of dirt road that was leading me back to the city.

We arrived in Cotonou late Friday afternoon after two days of travelling and one overnight stay in a shabby motel-type place along the route. My perspective completely changed during the nine months I had spent away from this city. In contrast to the dirty, smelly, unruly carnival I saw when I first got off the plane, I now saw a city full of life, restaurants, motels, opportunities for consumerism and consumption. I felt right at home. The driver delivered me to the door of the Peace Corps office. I paid him his fee and watched as his car disappeared into the crowded, chaotic, beautiful, wonderful, bustling streets of Cotonou.

I pounded on the huge metal doors to the gate that surrounded the Peace Corps compound. A Beninese man dressed in a military-style uniform let me in after verifying my identity with my Peace Corps id badge. The home office was westernized with its brick façade, black SUV's parked in neat rows, and air conditioning units blasting in several different places. There were coolers filled with ice and bottled water for the taking. This seemed like paradise to my weary mind and exhausted, sweaty, dust-caked body. This three-story building is where the directors of Peace Corps Benin worked, it also had rooms for volunteers to spend the night, a fully equipped kitchen, classrooms and conference rooms...it was kind of like a regular office building in the US. I entered the glass doors and walked to the "Book Room" at the end of the front hallway. The walls in this room were lined with bookshelves to the ceiling and they were filled with current novels to out-of-date textbooks. Volunteers were free to load up on these books as it was understood that there would be a lot of down time while waiting to work in the villages.

While I was in the process of choosing several worn paperbacks, I heard a familiar loud voice coming down the hall. I felt like fleeing the scene considering how horrible I must look right now fresh from the village and a two-day taxi ride. There was no escape. Brett entered the room wearing a perfectly white t-shirt, jeans, and a huge smile. "Lucy! You've escaped. I thought

I'd never see you again!"

He grabbed me for a big hug disregarding my hesitation, "Wait! I'm so dirty!"

"Oh Girl, I don't care. How the hell are you? What brings you to the big city?"

"I guess I just needed a break," I said, avoiding all the details about Hassaria that had recently weighed heavily on my emotions.

"Come with me. We are getting you a room, a shower, some real food, and a strong drink. You are going out on the town with me tonight because you have been working way too hard, girl." Brett had placed all my paperbacks back on the shelf and was leading me by the hand down the hallway.

We rode through chaotic streets on the backs of little mopeds to a big hotel, painted white, surrounded by palm trees and situated by a lake. There was a beautiful pool and beside it was an outside restaurant that served brick oven pizza. When we entered the lobby, Brett went to the desk to secure a room for me. I noticed a sitting area with four white wicker chairs, a white wicker couch, and a large coffee table. On the opposite side of the sitting area was a small boutique offering women's fashions for sale. The employees were overly helpful and generous; this was like actually being on vacation on some remote, exotic island.

Brett and I, accompanied by a concierge who insisted on carrying my one bag, rode the elevator to the third floor. My room was small but clean, sparkling white like everything else in this hotel. Paintings of African flora hung on every wall giving the white room multiple bursts of rich color. We walked onto the balcony and took in the view as the setting sun turned the shimmering lake different shades of red then quickly faded into black. "I can't believe I've been missing this. It's worth the wait though, I have to say."

"Lucy, you can't just disappear like you did for nine months. You have to enjoy your time here...two years is already flying by. It'll be over and you'll go back home never really knowing what this country is really about." Brett advised.

"You're right. I'm so thankful you showed up at the Peace Corps office. I don't know what I would be doing right now if you hadn't shown up when you did. I didn't really have a plan other than just coming here."

"You need a shower so hop to it. I've got plans for us. I'll be back in a few," Brett said leaving me standing on the balcony. I felt melancholy standing there alone watching this beautiful scene in this romantic setting. I wished for Connor to be standing beside me, squeezing my fingertips. The harsh truth is, however, the only reason I was standing in this faraway land on this beautiful balcony was because Connor wouldn't have me. Or even if he had changed his mind at the last minute with that cryptic message after my failed trip to see him, I had come all this way and this was my big drastic effort to get over him. Anyway, wasn't it time for me to be done with this tired, lingering first love nonsense? Wasn't it time my heart finally changed; opened up to new possibilities? I couldn't help feeling exiled from my own life; every feeling, every thought a contradiction. But this was supposed to be my recovery, my detox...my chance to let him go. "Hmm, maybe I just need more time," I said out loud for no one to hear.

While I was taking a hot shower and enjoying it beyond reason, Brett went to the hotel boutique and bought me a simple black sundress. "I love it. Thank you so much. But is it okay with my flip flops?" I asked worried that Brett would be concerned by my footwear.

"Lucy, you're in Africa. Let's not be vain," he said while applying gel to his perfectly coiffed hair. I rolled my eyes while slipping on my flip flops.

We sat poolside and ate brick oven pizza that was more delicious than any I had ever tasted and we each drank two glasses of wine. "So how do you look so great right now? I mean, you don't exactly look like you've been suffering through village life," I asked Brett after really noticing his tan smooth complexion and perfectly manicured nails.

"Honey, you can't let yourself go to hell just because you lack a few amenities. I have a country filled with beautiful men to impress and trust me, it's been working. And anyway, my village isn't really a village. It's more like a suburb. I'm in Cotonou every weekend."

"Oh, okay. I understand now. You certainly do have some amazing specimens to choose from. So how's that going...I mean, here in Africa?" I inquired suddenly curious about the gay scene in Benin.

"You'd be surprised. The men love me. You'll see. We're going out tonight and you just wait. I'm like a kid in a candy store, girl." "Whoa, Casanova, you're not doing anything dangerous... actually I meant to say, stupid, are you?" Brett shot me a look of disbelief. "Honey, this is eye-candy only. You can look but don't touch...well, maybe touch a little but I'm not stupid, Lucy. I know how to be safe." I was relieved to hear that but still sort of perplexed by this young gay man choosing to come to Africa for two years...it just seemed so out of character for the stereotype.

But then I remembered Andrew. I could clearly see him here trying to change the world for the better with his strong, innate, maternal instincts.

"Well, that's the kind of misinformation you get from stereotyping," I thought to myself.

I felt underdressed as our mopeds dropped us off by the curb in front of a big brick building boasting an enormous sign: NEW YORK NEW YORK. Brett tried to describe this place to me over dinner but words had failed him...or maybe I just didn't believe him. This place was like any club actually existing in New York City. There was a velvet rope, a door man, a line. I was shocked by the authenticity of this night club as each time the door opened, I could hear the music blasting and see the lights flashing. "God, I don't know if I have the energy for this," I thought to myself.

"Oh loosen up Lucy and get the hell inside," Brett scolded. Maybe I was thinking out loud.

When I walked in, I noticed that the club was built in concentric rings. The outer ring was the crowded bar. Then there were three steps leading down to the middle ring where there was a sitting area with big cushioned chairs and couches. The center ring was the huge dance floor situated around a giant mirrored pole.

The first song that blasted and beat its way right through my heart was Cher's "Believe." She was like a shaman leading me through and away from my nagging heartache. Her words empowered me, "Well, I know that I'll get through this 'cause I know that I am strong. And I don't need you anymore! I don't need you anymore! I don't need you anymore! No, I don't need you anymore!" I stood next to the dance floor drinking the colorful cocktails Brett had shoved in my hands feeling more carefree and empowered than I had ever felt.

"Isn't this amazing?" he yelled into my ear.

"Yes. I cannot believe this!" I yelled back.

"Come on!" Brett yelled and took my wrist. We were dancing on a crowded floor holding our drinks and each other while the DJ played a remix of my new personal anthem that seemed to go on forever. The club was filled with a multicultural mix of people all seemingly in love with each other and in love with life. This was such a contrast from Bello Tounga. I completely forgot about my tidy little village existing quietly in the pitch dark on the edge of the world.

The colorful drinks were going straight to my head. My flip flops had long been lost. I was dizzy with the lights, the music and the hands touching me in the humid mass of bodies.

I fell out of the crowd that had now turned to jumping up and down to the beat of another American techno mix and found my way to one of the couches. I was drunk and in need of supervision but my friend who had brought me here, and who was familiar with this place, was nowhere in sight. I must have looked like the most vulnerable naïve out-of-place Yovo... barefoot and euphoric with a helpless, uncontrollable grin on my numb face.

"Ce n'est pas bon. Tu es ivre," a tall, dark African said as he sat down beside me. He was dressed in jeans and a white button-down shirt... "not very African," I thought. "Et où sont tes chaussures?" he said pointing to my bare feet. My French seemed to have escaped with my sobriety. I began in English, "I don't know what you're saying. Do you speak Dendi? I speak Dendi." I laughed because I thought that was the most hilarious thing. "Non, mais je parle un peu d'anglais," he said. "Where do you go tonight?"

"What?" I said unable to interpret his broken English.

"You will leave here. Where do you go?"

"Oh, yeah, my friend and I are here together. He's here somewhere," I said looking around.

"I know him...American friend, Brett," he said laughing as if they were already old pals. "He is true African," he added with a proud smile. "Je m'appelle Mark. It is my Christian name."

"Bonjour. Je m'appelle Cher," I said out of my mind.

"Like singer? Cher?" he said, apparently buying it.

"Oui," was all I could manage.

"I come back. Don't go," he said and then headed for the bar. A minute or so later he handed me a drink, "It is only cola... will help you." His smile was huge and his teeth were blinding white.

"Merci, Christian," I said, getting his name hopelessly wrong while falling under the spell of this exotic French-speaking African man.

We sat on the couch trying to communicate but it was becoming more difficult since we were past the basics. We made our way onto the dance floor, all the while searching for Brett. He seemed to have left already which was extremely sobering. I felt deserted, a little pissed off, and a lot scared alone in the early hours of the morning in this Third World African city I was unfamiliar with. I took him by the hand and headed for the door so that we could try to communicate without yelling over the music. "Do you know where Brett is? I don't see him."

"Non. Maybe he go to hotel. I take you." He picked me up and carried me across the street (since I had no shoes) to where a couple of real motorcycles, not little taxi mopeds, were parked. He carefully put me down beside a big, shiny black and silver one. "Ici, pour toi," he said handing me his helmet. Beyond reason or common sense, I mounted this stranger's motorcycle and trusted him to take me to my hotel.

"Da Iquay baa," I quietly repeated climbing onto his big bike, trying to get control of my spinning head.

He cautiously navigated the streets of Cotonou while I hung onto him with all my might. On the way to the hotel, I took in the sites of the city. The skyline told a false tale: tall buildings that on closer inspection were only empty cinder block towers waiting for some kind of infrastructure, wiring, flooring, etc. The wide sidewalks of brick and stone were filled with vendors still trying to sell their odds and ends. Food stands were always busy selling meat, rice, fried plantains, and other less familiar things usually on sticks or wrapped in large green leaves. Men in yellow shirts sped their patrons on the backs of their mopeds to and fro even at three in the morning.

We pulled up to the front of the hotel and he parked his motorcycle. "Here you go," he said smiling, proud of getting his American phraseology correct. "Merci, umm, what was your name?" I said getting off his bike and handing him his helmet.

"Je m'appelle Mark. I like you, Cher" he said, giving me some sort of sultry-eyed seduction look.

"Well, merci. Okay? Je suis fatiguée. A bientôt," I said with my poor French, shaking my head and backing away into the hotel lobby, realizing I never told him my real name.

"How was your evening?" an employee asked. "Can I get you anything, ma'am?" he continued in his strong accent.

"Non, merci. Je suis...fine," I replied stumbling a little into the elevator. I rode it to the second floor where Brett's room was and knocked on his door. No one answered so I continued to my room on the third floor. "I can't believe Brett left me at that club. That was so dangerous," I fussed out loud to no one while changing into my night shirt. "I won't be doing that again." I lay back on my clean white sheets and watched the ceiling fan go round and round.

A few minutes later there was a quiet knock on my door. "Who is it?" I said expecting Brett's voice.

"C'est Mark." I jumped off the bed and scrambled to change back into my black sundress.

"Just a minute," I said not really thinking about whether or not he understood me. I opened the door slightly and said, "Oui?"

"Brett is waiting for you. Come." I closed the door just as he finished his statement and stood there holding the knob while I tried to decide if the old Lucy was going to be true to herself, decline the invitation for social interaction and go to bed or shrug her off and go meet Brett (I did have some choice words for him by the way). I cracked the door open and said, "une minute."

We walked to the elevator together. Mark said something in French that I did not understand and I let it pass without responding. The ride down was silent and awkward as I remembered his failed attempt to seduce me after bringing me to the hotel... "I like you, Cher." Just...don't.

I saw Brett sitting at a table under a thatch umbrella with several dark skinned people. I didn't know if they were African or European since Cotonou offered all kinds of ethnicities. Brett's French was better than mine since he used it pretty much one hundred percent of the time. I used Dendi more often but that was no use to me here. As I approached the table I could hear Brett and his friends speaking French and I felt ill-prepared... "Great. Another stressful social interaction and this time in a foreign language," I thought to myself. So I began in English, "Brett, hi, you left me."

"No, no. I didn't *really* leave you. I was there...just occupied. I got Mark to take care of you. Nice, huh?" he said eyeing Mark up and down.

"Wow. I don't know what to say, really. Thanks, I guess." I sat down beside Brett and Mark poured a wine glass to the top with something dark red.

"I looked for you before I left the club but you had already taken off with Mark. So, how did that go?" Brett asked.

"How did what go? The ride here? It was a little scary actually considering I was at the mercy of a complete stranger in a city I don't know."

"Oh relax, honey. Mark is a perfect gentleman. I would have freaked out if you had left with anyone else. Trust me. Anyway, tomorrow, I'm taking you on a little road trip to my village. I think you'll love it."

"Okay. Sorry about freaking out...I'm just not used to..."

Brett interrupted me, "No, you're right. I should have stayed with you. It's my fault...really. I'm sorry I disappeared on you. And it's not what you think, Lucy. I was mostly outside talking to one of my adult students. He's desperate to learn English and talks my ears off every time he sees me," he said with a roll of his eyes and a grin as he reached over, grabbed my chin and planted a kiss on my cheek. I smiled and drank what Mark had poured in my glass trying to just relax; it was sweet, cold, and smooth.

"We're waiting for the sun to come up. That's when we sleep

on the weekends in Cotonou," Brett said. Some of the men at the table laughed and agreed which let me know they could speak, or at least understand, English. "Well, I'm going to miss out on seeing that this morning because I'm about to pass out. I'm going to bed now. You know where I'll be," I said to Brett as I stood up to leave.

"Oh no. Cher, you must stay for sunrise," Mark said, grabbing my hand.

"Cher?" Brett said with an understandable dose of confusion and a coy smile.

"Never mind. I was drunk, ok."

I pulled my hand away from his strong grip and made my way to the comfortable, clean bed in the chilly room where I did not need a mosquito net. I lay there longing to hear wood cracking and popping in small fires. I missed the quiet murmurings of the village elders and the star show twinkling in the black sky. "What is happening to me?" I wondered, realizing that I actually missed my beautiful village and its quiet existence beyond the fringe of civilization. I turned on my side and wondered what Connor would think if he knew where I was and what I was doing. I almost drifted off smiling, hugging my pillow imagining him beside me, before I reprimanded myself, "No, no, no. At least try to let him go. At least try. At least try," I repeated in whispers as I fell asleep. Africa was changing me in *almost* every way.

I woke up when Brett knocked on my door. I looked over at my watch, 11:30am. "Hi. Did you even get any sleep?" I questioned while letting him into my room. He was dressed in a pair of khaki shorts and a light blue polo.

"Yes, of course. I sleep like a baby when I'm here. Let's get you ready. Here you go; I bought you a pair of flip flops from the boutique since you somehow lost yours on the dance floor. That's classic, Lucy," he said chuckling.

"Yeah, that was really terrible, I know," I said. "Thanks."

We ate breakfast at a little roadside stand. One man was running the show behind a bar, under a sheet of metal with two hot plates and a few pots and pans. He was selling egg sandwiches on baguette rolls and instant coffee with sweetened condensed milk. It was delicious…more delicious than the day-old rice or millet patties and warm water I would usually have for breakfast in Bello Tounga.

Brett was excited for me to visit his village where cinder block homes and stores with tin roofs and metal doors lined dirt roads. His home actually had a screened in front porch, a working shower, and electrical outlets that allowed him to sleep by the breeze of an oscillating fan. He explained, "My home is a little more privileged than most since I'm the Yovo teacher."

"Yeah, mine is too," I replied thinking about my cement slab with the thatch fencing and my private latrine and bucket bath.

"This is our school," he said as we approached a large cement building with two big metal doors.

"Very nice," I replied as he unlocked the doors so we could go inside. I was noticing the mounted chalk board, the desks, the notebooks and textbooks when Brett said, "What is your school like, Lucy, way out in no-man's land?"

"Brett, all I can really say is that it is very different. My school is under a tree. My students sit on the ground after we sweep it clean of dirt. We are only learning French. It's like I'm not even really teaching…not like you are here," I said taking a seat in one of the wooden desks and noticing the well-used soccer field outside of the huge window.

"I know it's hard. Bello Tounga is the farthest village from Cotonou and therefore one of the most difficult. You should feel proud about getting that post. It means they think you can handle it."

"I never really thought of it that way. I mean, maybe you're right. It's just hard for me to reprogram my idea of daily accomplishments, you know."

"I can't imagine. Damn, girl, it's hard for me to do that here. Lucy, honestly, I would have freaked out if they assigned me to live that far away from civilization...from the city. I think they must have known better," Brett said erasing some lesson he had written on the chalkboard during his last class.

I smiled at his honesty and wondered what it was that made the Peace Corps directors think I could handle it. I figured it must have been the God's at work again knowing it would take an extreme experience to help me get over Connor. After all, I came here in need of drastic measures and Bello Tounga offered them up on a daily basis.

"I love your village and your house, Brett. Your school is amazing too. You're right. It is like living in a suburb. It's such a great assignment," I said on our way back to the hotel.

"I love it too. I feel very lucky," Brett said with a smile.

"I have to say, though, as rough as it is to live in Bello Tounga, it has shoved its way into my heart. I love the kids I teach and the elders are so wise and set in their ways...in their culture. But there are some things that will haunt me forever. I mean it can be a very brutal place." I told Brett about Hassaria and Amedu.

"That's awful. My students are all Christian and they all speak

French already. It's like two different worlds isn't it?"

"My village definitely is a different world compared to here," I agreed.

"Girl, we need some drinks after that story," he said lifting the mood.

"And some brick oven pizza," I added. After a few silent seconds, I said, "Hey Brett, do you know where I can get a soccer ball and some paper tablets and pencils?"

"Of course, we'll stock up when we get back into the city," he replied.

I spent one more night in Cotonou before I squeezed into the backseat of a taxi with three other adults, a cumbersome soccer ball, and a large bag full of paper tablets and pencils. The driver was going to take me almost halfway and then I'd have to get another taxi to carry me the rest of the way to Bello Tounga since most drivers were unwilling to go that far off the beaten path.

Traveling in Benin was (and most likely still is) a horror story so I won't digress into the four days it actually took to get back to my village, the two breakdowns, the thirty or so miles we sped down the dusty road on a flat tire, the unexpected two-nights sleeping in the house of a family I did not know, or the endless hours of bargaining and waiting for a driver to agree to take too much of my money in return for delivering me all the way to Bello Tounga. Once I arrived back to my little village tucked away from the rest of the world on the edge of a life-sustaining river, it is not hard to see why I rarely ever left again until my service ended.

CHAPTER 33

After my return from the city, the children of Bello Tounga stayed busy learning French in the morning and doing chores in the afternoon. Then, before sunset, they rushed to the soccer field on the outskirts of the village with their new ball and played until it was dark. I stayed busy teaching French and just trying to survive the heat, the mosquitoes, the lack of food, and the reality of warm drinking water.

My students came to the cement patio each night but it never was the same after Hassaria left. Amedu never showed up again either. Although more and more students eventually came to my nighttime tutoring sessions, none of them could ever replace those two. I saw firsthand how difficult Hassaria's life was going to be because girls were forced to come to Bello Tounga for the same reason she was forced to leave; to get married to strangers. They always looked worried and afraid. I never saw one young bride look happy in her new life.

After seeing the bounty of supplies for students at Brett's school, I felt challenged to provide more for mine. Even though I brought enough paper tablets and pencils back from Cotonou to last my students at least two years, I wanted them to have a way to earn a little money so they could go to the market and buy paper tablets and pencils even after I was gone. The most sustainable way for them to continually have a little money was to plant fruit-bearing trees in an enclosed orchard; that way they could pick the fruit and sell it at the market each week. I wrote a proposal to my director and received money to buy thirty young orange trees, ten metal watering buckets, and materials to build a fence out of wooden stakes and wire to keep the animals from destroying the saplings.

The village elders approved of the plan and gladly gave us the land adjacent to our outside school to build the orchard. Over the course of three months, pickup trucks would randomly arrive at Bello Tounga with trees and fencing supplies. There was excitement among the villagers with each delivery; it was like Christmas with the adults standing back clapping and the children running around screaming with delight while holding metal watering buckets above their heads like trophies. The entire village took pride in helping build this orchard.

We planted the trees as they arrived and built the fence as quickly as possible. Although these young trees would not bear fruit for a few years, my students still had the pride of accomplishment, the satisfaction of knowing they had planted an orchard and it belonged to them.

In Africa, it's about looking to the future anyway. There, hope is a way of life, and our little orchard provided a great deal of it. I wonder if that orchard is still standing or if time and neglect have successfully plotted against it. I can only hope those trees, now a decade old, are standing tall, filling an abundance of baskets with oranges, providing a little money for the students of Bello Tounga to buy their own paper tablets and pencils.

Days persisted in the beautiful village by the edge of the river just as they had for centuries. On very rare occasions, something would happen to stir up the dust, dent the bubble, reroute the current. Before the sun set on this random day that promised to fit right into the normal pattern of life, a black SUV with the Peace Corps emblem on the door pulled up to the village stirring the dust and re-routing the current. The children burst into urgent cries of "HASSIA, HASSIA, E MA KA!!" insisting that I "COME NOW!" I was all the way down by the river washing my laundry when I heard them yelling. I scrambled up the embankment to see what the fuss was about and knew something was wrong as soon as I saw the truck. One of the Peace Corps directors, an American man, was already standing in the village surrounded by excited children when I approached.

"Hi Lucy. Can we go somewhere to talk...in private?"

"Well, we can go into my hut here, but I don't know how much privacy we'll get."

His expression let me know he understood. We walked inside and he handed over a sheet of paper. It had written on it: "Robert William Bells, deceased, July 10, 1997, Heart Failure."

I looked up at him and said, "It's the fifteenth, right? It's actually his birthday today."

"Lucy, I am so sorry to have to bring this news to you. I know this is very difficult to hear being so far away from your family." He put his arm around my shoulders and continued, "We can work with you quickly if you want to go home although his funeral was yesterday, Sunday. You only have about six months left of service; you can end early without penalty if you want to."

I turned to face him still holding the letter, "I'm not leaving. I can't." I looked over at the shabby screen door that was about to fall from its hinges; four dirty little faces were looking in at us in complete amazement. "I knew my dad was really sick before I left. I'm not surprised by this news. It's just...I don't know... heavy. I wasn't there for his funeral. It's weird."

"When your mother called, she said you wouldn't want to leave," he said with a half-smile. "She also said that she understands why...and so does everyone at home."

"Thank you for coming here to let me know. It's not an easy journey," I said.

"Of course, Lucy. I'm just sorry it took so long to get you the message; we had several delays along the way. Is there anything I can get for you...have sent up here for you? Do you need anything?"

I really didn't know what to say. There was so much need here but it was up to Mother Nature to provide for Bello Tounga... not us. "No, thanks. We are doing okay," I said. "Da Iquay baa," I added.

"What was that?" he said with a look of surprise at my natural use of the language.

"It's our motto here: 'if it's the Will of God.'"

"Well, Lucy, it looks as if you have done a great job immersing yourself in their culture. I saw your orchard on the way in...it looks great. You seem to have done an outstanding job being the ambassador Peace Corps needs you to be. We are proud of you."

"Thank you, Sir."

We stepped out of my hut and within a few minutes, a crowd of children disappeared in a thick cloud of dust as they chased the big black truck down the long dirt road.

I met with the elders who wanted to know what the visit was about. I let them know in the only way my Dendi would allow, "Hi Ba koy Iquay foo." Literal translation: "My father has gone to God's house." This phrase was sufficient. They understood and surrounded me, putting their hands on my head, shoulders, and back while they prayed out loud, all at once.

A celebration for the passing of my father commenced on the next day and lasted a week. There was dancing and drumming in circles. The stamina of the men holding those little drums under their arms in the scorching heat was otherworldly as they kept the beat going for hours and hours. Young girls and the occasional show-off older woman jumped into the drum circle and ferociously stomped the earth, bent over, arms flailing, head bobbing, eyes rolling. Women set up big, black cauldrons in the middle of the village and cooked more food than was necessary, including a goat that was killed in my dad's honor.

Death was not just another part of life in Bello Tounga; it was an occasion to celebrate passing through this difficult life into the next; hopeful that it would be an easier existence. I celebrated the passing of my father like a true African, hoping his next go 'round would be easier on him, if that's how it works. Hope as a way of life – a philosophy my fellow villagers and I deeply shared. I just couldn't fathom the depths of hope that lived in their hearts...especially when the rains began to fall.

CHAPTER 34

Weeks passed slowly while the familiar beat of life in Bello Tounga took back its ancient rhythm. The rainy season was on its way which meant repairing and fortifying mud huts was the priority on almost everyone's list of chores. After our French lessons under the baobab tree, my students hurried home to get machetes and ropes; they had to collect wood, straw, and any other materials that could be used to prepare their mud huts for the torrential rains moving in slowly, mercilessly over Bello Tounga.

The only villagers not on hut duty were a few women who cooked all day preparing reserves of food. While two of them pounded dry millet and corn into flour, the rest stood over black cauldrons of boiling water stirring in that pounded flour for hours on end; exhausting work. The result was a thick, sticky substance that looked like mashed potatoes but tasted like fermented hell. I was taught early on in my service how to properly eat this substance they called pâte (pronounced "pot"): scoop up a glob with my pointer and middle fingers, dip it into some kind of oily or slimy sauce, and slap it on my tongue. It would slide down my throat in one slick lump. For me, this was eating out of necessity but the villagers loved it. Besides, pâte could be stored conveniently in big pots and small bowls and would easily last through the rainy season.

The first soaking lasted six days by my count. I stayed inside except for my necessary trips to the latrine. The thatch fencing all blew over and soaked into a mushy, muddy mess. Animals huddled together under their inadequate shelters. We all stayed hunkered down in our huts for days while the clouds unleashed an ungodly amount of rain that fell steady and heavy like an endless shower. The days were dark and dreary. Children sat around with their parents singing and playing hand games. They were already accustomed to this part of their lives. I spent much of this time alone except for the occasional visitor who would dart through the torrent, knock on the wooden part of my screen door, and then let themselves in. I brushed up on Dendi during these visits and became somewhat conversational in my ability to speak it.

I read books and wrote in my journals during the many rainy hours I spent alone. I wrote about Bello Tounga, heartfelt ramblings about my dad's tragic life, and plans for the future. I made lists of food I wanted to eat and places I wanted to visit when I returned home. Connor showed up in only one statement: *"I don't know if I will achieve my original goal for coming here because even after all I have done and experienced, after all the ways Africa has opened my eyes and changed me, I still only imagine sharing it with him. God, what is wrong with me???"*

As the sun rose on the seventh day, the clouds broke and a crystal clear blue sky appeared above us. Everyone came out of their shelters. Children splashed in puddles, men and women checked their homes for damage, and everyone did their part to collect rainwater from any source above the ground. As I watched from my patio, villagers milled around and socialized during this break from Mother Nature but they knew she had more in store.

In the early morning hours on the eighth day, torrential rains began to fall again. I was sleeping in my hut on my mattress safe and secure within my mosquito net when I was awakened by a terrible cacophony of sounds. Thunder was booming overhead. Heavy rain was falling. My neighbors' hut had crashed in on top of them and the family was screaming and trying to scramble everyone to safety in the soaking wet pitch dark. Everyone who heard the commotion came out of their huts to see what was happening. It was hard to see in the darkness but it was apparent that the entire hut had been reduced to a pile of mud.

One of the women, Nafisa, was in hysterics crawling over the muddy pile, frantically digging with her hands. I gathered enough information from the crowd to learn that her baby was still in there; still under all that mud. Several villagers, including myself, climbed onto the pile and helped her dig through the mud as desperately as we could. It was clear that our efforts were futile but we had to try. Just two weeks ago, we had celebrated Saidatu's birth with the killing of a goat and a drum circle. I had seen Nafisa take the razor-sharp edge of a smooth, chiseled stone and cut three gashes on both of her baby's cheeks. She had scarred her daughter before life had a chance to and now her baby was gone, buried in a pile of mud.

Two more weeks of rain fell before the clouds broke, allowing a more normal pattern of life to emerge. It was like the village was waking up after a long hibernation, like life was slowly starting up again. Elders were coming out to assess the damage; men were repairing what the rains had affected, while the women were tending to everything else. Several of my students and I hurried through the mud to check on our orchard. Although a few stakes of the fence had blown over, it was mostly unharmed. We jumped up and down and ran around the orchard yelling, thanking "Iquay" for his mercy.

Nafisa's baby was eventually recovered. Her little body was wrapped in colorful fabric and carried to a deep hole her father had dug on the outskirts of the village. All able-bodied women and children of Bello Tounga walked to the burial site in a straight line singing a chant that I did not know while Nafisa, carrying her baby, lead the way. Deezay spoke a few hopeful words sending Saidatu on her way to an easier existence, then the infant was carefully placed in the hole by her mother. After the hole was filled in, some of us placed river reeds, flowering weeds, and bottle-cap toys on the broken earth to mark her grave. We returned to the village walking in a straight line just as we had come.

It was understood that since the village had just taken a beating from Mother Nature, Saidatu's passing-on celebration would be minimal; drums for a day and two chickens for the family. Nafisa's culture expected that she would have several more children since she was young. It was practically normal for the first or second born not to survive. I never saw Nafisa cry about Saidatu's death, but I had seen her full of fear, panicking, and desperate, as she dug through the mud searching for her baby in the pouring down darkness. I wondered how she really felt; if she wanted to return to the village where she had grown up and cry on her own mother's shoulder.

The last day of my service as a Peace Corps volunteer arrived without fanfare - no drumming circle or sacrificial goat. It just arrived and I left the beautiful village by the river like it wasn't my home. I had the day circled on my calendar but one of my students who was fascinated by the pictures, "Natural Wonders of the United States," had taken it to show his family some time ago. Of course, I never saw it again. That morning I swept the ground with my little helpers and drew a fresh square under our baobab tree. I taught French to the seventeen students who showed up for class, and then we weeded the orchard and repaired fencing. I ate rice and fish for lunch sitting on my cement patio.

When the black SUV pulled up, it dawned on me; today is the day I leave Bello Tounga. I sat frozen with mixed emotions. The children were yelling and jumping with excitement around the big, black vehicle that had come to take their teacher, their friend away. Just as I finally felt like I fit into their pattern of life, it was time for me to leave.

A Beninese man who worked for the Peace Corps office in Cotonou made the trip to Bello Tounga to retrieve me. He approached me on my patio and spoke to me in English, heavy with an African-French accent, "Good afternoon, Miss Lucy. My name is David. I have come to take you to Cotonou. It is time to go home." I stood up and shook hands with him not really knowing what to say. "Shall I begin loading?" he asked, peeking into my tidy but unpacked hut. "I have boxes in the truck for you."

"No thanks. I don't need them. I didn't know this was my day. I haven't even told anyone I'm leaving." I walked into my hut and quickly gathered a few items: my panyas, journals, letters from home, and drawings from my students. I placed them in my duffle bag and walked out of my mud hut for the last time.

While David loaded the butane gas tank, the double burner, and my bag into the truck, I walked through the village surrounded by my students and my village family. I told them in my best Dendi that I was going home to my family in America and that another teacher would soon come to take my place. We hugged and said our goodbyes with smiles on our faces. I heard "Da Iquay baa" a hundred or more times as it spread throughout the crowd.

Elders watched as the SUV pulled away. I watched from the back seat as my students ran with all their might in a thick cloud of dust behind the truck until they each fell out of the race. Tears started flowing as Anafey, the last little dust-covered boy, running with his hands outstretched, disappeared from view as he fell flat on the ground. And just that quickly, Bello Tounga became a part of my past.

"David, please don't mind me; I'm just a little emotional right now," I said with tears streaming down my cheeks. I bent over with my face in my hands and cried, releasing the built-up emotions from spending the last two years of my life in the most extreme environment I could imagine. I was crying because I would miss my students and the beautiful village by the river. I felt like I hadn't accomplished enough for them, and now it was over, just like that....I cried for their lives. While I had so much to look forward to, the people of Bello Tounga would be stuck in the same bubble, the same current, putting the same pieces of the puzzle together time and time again. There is tragedy and sweet simplistic beauty in my memories of this village. I also cried because I was relieved it was over. I missed my family, food, hot showers, and blue jeans. It was time for me to get back to putting the pieces of my own puzzle together.

David drove us straight through, only stopping for food, drinks, and short naps. When we arrived at the office in Cotonou, I signed a few papers and was given a certificate of completion as well as seven hundred US dollars in a white envelope (money that was given to all volunteers at the end of their service to help with the big transition back to America). I rode on the back of a taxi-moped to the hotel by the lake and slept soundly in the clean white air-conditioned room where I did not need a mosquito net. Instead of dreaming about the indulgences I would soon have at home, I dreamed about lying on my mattress under the stars, wood popping and cracking in small fires, the low murmurings of Dendi lulling me to sleep in a far-off distant land.

Two years of living in a remote village in Africa can change a person's view on life, work, the world, humanity. While flying west over the Atlantic Ocean back to a home from which I felt disconnected and estranged, I was aware that Africa had certainly changed me, well, mostly. There was one remnant left of that naïve girl who had run so far away from home; it was buried underneath the debris of a still-broken heart. All that was left intact was Connor.

****

I wonder how Bello Tounga has changed since I left almost fifteen years ago; probably not very much. There is still too much heat and rain at one time. They are still rebuilding the same mud huts that are now at least a century old. Children with scarred faces now have babies of their own to scar, and old men are still delaying Peace Corps volunteers with lengthy salutations. I arrived in a village already in progress; no more than a ghost just passing through. My bewildered eyes and soft, sanitary hands offered help knowing full well the calloused, dirty, sickly children who stared back at me in awe were more equipped to survive than I. I depended on them and survived only by their mercy, or pity. I was there for adventure and escape from a just-south-of-perfect life. They were born there. Abject poverty, Harmattan, mud huts, rainy season, unbearable heat, malarial mosquitoes, parasitic water, and occasional lack of food; this was their home. I wonder how those souls ended up there. Maybe God deals the cards in heaven and if your hand doesn't add up, your soul gets Bello Tounga; trapped by the endless and tormented tangle of dirt roads and the inhumane climate of a disadvantaged location on the globe. I wonder, though, if my hand added up. My soul got the American Southeast: air conditioner, vacations, vaccinations, clean running water, indoor plumbing, paved roads, microwave ovens, ice, and cable TV. But I was born with my own personal disadvantage as limiting and stifling as theirs: consistency. I grow older, but my heart refuses to change.

CHAPTER 35

"What we once enjoyed and deeply loved
we can never lose,
For all that we love deeply becomes a part of us."

Helen Keller

The plane arrived in Washington D.C. around 6am. I could see from the window that it was snowing a little. My body was bracing for the shock of below-freezing temperatures after spending two years in African heat. Mom, Mary, and Tory were at the airport waiting to pick me up. We hugged for a long time, each telling me how happy she was that I was finally home. Trying to hide mixed feelings about that, I just smiled and said, "Thanks. It's great to see you." Mom had the idea to bring one of my coats, a pair of jeans, and a sweatshirt. I was grateful for this since I arrived in flip flops, a panya, and a t-shirt.

We ate breakfast in a diner. The smell was intoxicating. I ordered and then devoured a tall stack of pancakes dripping with melted butter and maple syrup, four strips of bacon, and coffee with cream. My stomach ached from being stretched so far so fast. Mary warned that I might need to take it easy for a while before I just dive in like that. It was good advice but I didn't care. I had been hungry for this for two years.

On the way to our hotel, I saw a CVS Pharmacy and asked Mom to pull into the parking lot. She waited in the car while Mary, Tory, and I went inside. "I don't even know where to start. This is so overwhelming," I said looking around with amazement.

"Lucy, it's not like you didn't spend all your life around this stuff. You've just been gone for two years," Mary said trying to bring some perspective to my digression into some sort of modern-day Mowgli straight from the jungle.

"I know, it's weird but this just feels so strange to have so many choices of so many things at my fingertips. I'll never take it for granted again...ever."

We purchased four diet sodas in plastic bottles, two handfuls of string cheese, one large bag of barbeque potato chips, two large bags of M&M's and two king-sized Butterfingers. I also bought two pairs of socks, a scarf, and a bag of underwear.

Our hotel room was warm and cozy – a stark contrast to the last hotel room I stayed in with its cool breeze from the ceiling fan and sheer curtains billowing in from the open balcony doors. I admit that I felt out of place here. Coming home to America after living so far from civilization proved to be just as shocking to the senses as arriving in Benin had been two years ago.

After I took a hot shower and put on my warm clothes, we talked for hours in the hotel room about my African experience. It was difficult assigning words and phrases to describe my life in Bello Tounga because they all came out sounding so tragic and awful. I must have seemed insane telling about the hardships I faced while also trying to explain my connection and love for the people and the village, my sadness at leaving, and my desire to go back someday.

"You really have to go through it to understand the Peace Corps motto, 'the toughest job you'll ever love.' It took me a while but it finally sunk in," I said pulling out my students' drawings from my bookbag. "This one is our school, under the baobab tree. And this is the orchard we built. This one is about hope...you see, he is standing beside a big basket of oranges to sell at the market. The oranges won't grow for another three years but he is already excited for the first harvest. This one is a drawing of our tutoring sessions on my cement patio and this one is of the children playing soccer at night. These are some cards they made me when Dad died...you see the drum circle and the women making food." The children's drawings did a much better job conveying the beauty and difficulty of life in Bello Tounga than my words ever could.

****

Sitting in the passenger seat beside Mom on the way home to North Carolina, I made a list of urgent things to do:

1. *Go home, go through stuff, give most of it away*
2. *Visit Dad's gravesite*
3. *Go to mountains for a week*
4. *Apply for teaching positions in Chapel Hill*
5. *Look for work until I get a teaching job*
6. *Look for place to live*

Mary and Tory followed behind us from Washington so that I could go with them to the mountains after I collected my things from the trailer and visited Dad's grave. That already took care of numbers one through three on my list. "Back to business as usual," I thought. What took a day and a half in America would have likely taken a month and a half in Bello Tounga.

I asked Mary to go to the cemetery with me. "Should we say a little prayer for him?" I asked.

"Sure," Mary said grabbing my hand.

We stood there silently for a moment and then I began, "Dear God, Let Dad's soul rest in peace. He knew so little of it while he was living. And please forgive him for taking out his anger on us and help us to forgive him as well. Amen."

Mary and I kissed the backs of our fingers and laid them on his tombstone for a few seconds. We walked away while she told me details about the small funeral. I was touched to hear that Andrew had come. She also mentioned that Trudi sent a sympathy card. My stomach dropped and my face turned red as the blood rushed to my head with the sudden acceleration of my heartbeat. "This is not a good sign," I thought to myself.

"Lucy, are you okay?" Mary asked when she noticed my reaction. "Are you upset about Dad or is it the mention of Connor's mother that has you all red in the face?"

"I can't help it. I can't help my body's reactions. And yes, it is the mention of Trudi. I haven't really thought about trying to contact her for a while. You know, I was supposed to be over him by now but I don't think I am."

"Of course you're not. You need to read her card though. It might help."

"Oh God. Don't tell me he's married again," I said making presumptions.

"Wow, Lucy, what would make you think that?"

"Sarcasm? Really?"

"Sorry. It's just that I don't know which is more ridiculous, his addiction to getting married, or your addiction to him." She left me speechless because she was right. There was no retort I could fathom to argue her point. We rode home discussing our trip to the mountains and my plans for the immediate future; everything except for the only thing that was on my mind.

****

Dear Joan,

I am so sorry to hear of Bobby's passing and thank you for the card letting me know. He certainly suffered through his illnesses for many years. In some cases, it seems like death is a blessing for the one who doesn't have to suffer anymore.

Is Lucy still in Africa? If so, I wonder how she will deal with the news so far away from home. I remember when Connor came home from Saudi Arabia and found out about his grandfather's death. Those days seem so distant from us now.

On a related topic, Connor is getting married again this spring in Hawaii. Our family is taking a little vacation and they decided to wait and do it there. She's a nice girl from our hometown and we are just hoping this one will bring him some stability and happiness. I don't think he has ever loved any of his girlfriends or wives for that matter the way he loved Lucy, but what do I know? He has graduated from college with his Associate's degree in something dealing with business. I don't pretend to understand.

I pray for Lucy's safe return and hope to hear from her when she comes home from this big adventure.

Love and peace to your family,

Trudi

I was kind of proud of myself: no tears, no hysterics, no screaming or ripping apart the card. I just sat there on Mom's bed beside Mary and said, "Hawaii...how cliché."

"I know. It's embarrassing; marriage number three and the family is celebrating in Hawaii. I hope they have a good time while it lasts," Mary said banking on my outward disguise of calloused, bulletproof, ironclad emotions. She took Trudi's card and put it in the drawer to Mom's bedside table. "Let's get your stuff together and get on the road. I can't wait for you to see our new bakery."

CHAPTER 36

I couldn't help feeling nostalgic when we entered the Blue Ridge Region of North Carolina. I had come this way with Jason during my college years, but my mind was flooded with memories of another trip; one I had made with Connor years before. My lips formed a melancholy smile and my eyes filled with tears while a breathy chuckle escaped. I closed my eyes and savored the image of speeding around the tight curves with New Order blasting. I imagined looking beside me and seeing him, Connor Hawthorn, before life, well, before I, broke his heart. I thought to myself, "He can continue to look, but he will never find a love as pure and perfect as ours. No matter how many wives come and go he will always be searching for me. And I'll be ready when he comes back." This is my mantra, my hope, my brick wall, my obsession, my ball and chain. This is my curse.

And so time, nor distance, nor drastic measures had changed my heart. I came home from Africa as determined as ever to be there - ready and waiting - when Connor finally realized that he couldn't survive without me.

****

GOTHIC SO GOOD Bakery and Coffee: they finally did it. Mary and Tory had saved a little money and acquired a business loan to buy a small two-room wooden house with a wrap-around front porch right on the edge of their quaint mountain town. Within a year, the inside had been remodeled and the kitchen appliances installed. Tables and chairs sat atop floral rugs and local art randomly hung about adding an eclectic vibe to the adorable little space. The only thing gothic about the place was the music playing from the mounted speakers and the young kids hanging out downing too many cups of coffee with their tattoos, spiked hair, black clothes, and artistic ways. Mary and Tory were always giving them advice on how to truly be gothic since they were considered "old school Goths" by this time.

My week in the mountains was busy. I helped out at the bakery and learned how to make my favorite "Boys Don't Cry Cupcakes." The recipe was a simple four, three, two, one mixture but on the inside, there was a sweet wasabi cream cheese surprise that would bring tears to most any boy, girl, man, or woman for that matter. The vanilla buttercream icing was also topped with crushed wasabi peas. This cupcake brought tears to my eyes at least once every day that I stayed in the mountains.

I was also busy finding a job as a teacher in Chapel Hill. I thought it might be more complicated, but all it took was one phone call to human resources. After a background check and a faxed resume, I was hired as a long-term substitute (this took care of number four on my list which meant that number five was no longer needed). A ninth-grade American Literature teacher was out on maternity leave for the rest of the year and I could start next Monday. It was Wednesday, two days before my twenty-fifth birthday, and things were falling into place. On Thursday, I called Chapel Hill Reality and secured a one-bedroom apartment close to campus (number six – my entire list – complete!). Friday night, we celebrated.

People started to arrive around six o'clock. The house was lit with candles and decorated with light blue and white streamers. "Happy Birthday" banners were taped to the walls. Mary baked two dozen of my favorite cupcakes while Tory baked a birthday cake.

"This is so great. I haven't really celebrated my birthday in a long time," I said stuffing my mouth with some delicious morsel and then washing it down with a cold beer.

"We know!" they said in unison.

"Wow, you guys are hilarious. You're, like, becoming the same person."

"WE KNOW!" they said again in unison, bursting into laughter.

The party lasted well into the night with people coming and going, dancing, drinking, and eating. I was introduced to several people who asked me questions like, "How was it in Africa? Was it hot? How'd you use the bathroom? Did you have to eat insects?" I tried to respond intellectually, but my beer-infused mind limited me to one word per question: "Crazy. Yes. Outside. No."

Then they would hug me and kiss me on the cheek like we were old friends. "This is how we do here in Blackrock, Lucy. Just embrace it," Mary said, laughing at my stressed expression while pulling me into the middle of the room to dance.

"My favorite Smith's song ever!" I said as "Stop Me If You Think You've Heard This One Before" began to play.

"I know!" Mary said turning it up all the way. "That's why I put this CD in the rotation. You used to listen to it all the time!" We danced and sang along with Morrissey as I lost myself to the bittersweet nostalgia of years gone by.

I was happy to be home, with my sister, in my own culture. I was happy. And that is how I began my twenty-fifth year, dancing with my sister and Tory in the mountains to my favorite music; two days from working and living in Chapel Hill...Connor Hawthorn clearly and unmistakably a fixture on my horizon. I was sure that when he heard I was home from Africa he would come back to me.

I still loved him; Africa could not change that. My body still only wanted his and my eyes still only saw his beauty. The magic behind the message was real; he was coming back because he belonged to me and I belonged to him. Even though he was about to make another mistake with another woman, I didn't care because I knew it wouldn't last and I would be ready when he came back.

****

But five years can pass in the blink of an eye...and then five more are gone before you know it. I've been teaching American Literature to high school students and I've earned my master's degree. I am currently working on my doctorate. I'll be a Doctor of Education and then, hopefully, I'll work on campus for the remainder of my days...that is until Connor comes back and we figure the rest out together.

I wrote to his mother once a few years back. Months passed before she responded but her little card finally came, out of the blue. The part I read over and over said:

"Connor is divorced from his last wife and has promised to stay

232

single for a long while if not forever. He is off on some crazy adventure in South America, climbing rocks and forging through the rainforest. I worry about him. He keeps searching for something that's just beyond his reach."

Well, I've always known what he was searching for. And I'm right here. I'm ready. All he has to do is find his way back to me.

I've been living in a little white house with a front porch and a swing for six years now. You might remember this little house – I spent many nights here with Jason when I was in college. It was for sale and I couldn't pass it up. There are a lot of memories here and they are good ones. I've taken my time decorating but it's coming along. Since I don't have many visitors, my red couch and my floral armchair are sufficient for sitting. Every once in a while, I'll invite a colleague over for dinner and we'll sit at my dining room table discussing work, current affairs, or whatever comes up.

At the end of the day, I'm happy with my little white house, and I'm happy with my work. In fact, I'm happy with my life, well mostly. I visit my favorite little bakery in the mountains each fall and spring. I vacation in the Outer Banks with Mom, Mary, and Tory each summer. I have a fat, lazy cat who relentlessly tries to keep me from my work. I even flew to Paris for a week with Mary and Tory two years ago. I stood under the Eiffel Tower, rode a boat up the Seine, and spent six nights in a tiny room in a little hotel with shutters that opened out to a beautiful view of the city. Each night I cried into my pillow because I wanted Connor to be there beside me, holding me, sharing this experience with me. I am mostly happy until the doubt creeps in and I see a future where there is no Connor, but instead, a lonely, old lady still holding out for some childish notion.

I sit at my table a lot these days working on my dissertation and grading essays. Ever since I finished my letter to Connor, I've been getting a great deal more accomplished. I used to be distracted by all the things I needed to tell him spinning in my head like words sloshing around in a basin of water, randomly surfacing in no particular order or thought pattern. But I think I finally got it right. And like the letter says, he'll probably never read it, but at least it's there, in writing, just in case.

It's been almost twenty years since I've seen him and there is a part of me that is beginning to lose hope. That scares me since hope has been my way of life for ...well, way too long. So for now, all I can do is just what I've always done since Connor left me standing on the corner lot - continue to wait for the magic behind the message to bring him back to me, or for my heart to decide it's finally time to let him go.

CHAPTER 37

"The course of true love never did run smooth."
A Midsummer Night's Dream
-Shakespeare

It's been months since I sat at my dining room table and opened this file on my computer. In fact, it's almost been a year since I've even looked at this document, this book that tells my story, but that's only because I've been patiently waiting for...you know. Not one event has happened that would add texture, flavor, plot or depth to what I have already written - that is until recently.

My story finally has an ending and I will attempt to tell you how I have come to understand the true nature of the fireflies that returned to my backyard each summer; the fireflies that taught me about letting go and coming back; that taught me about hope and patience.

****

As winter's subtle exit gave way to the colorful awakening of spring and the thick air of summer thinned out to crisp sweater weather, a little magic was brewing in my stars. It was drizzling and chillier than normal on that fall afternoon. I had just poured myself a big glass of Merlot and was about to plant myself on my red couch for the rest of the day with a fat cat, a cozy blanket, and Heathcliff and Catherine (needing to dwell on a love story that wasn't my own for a change.) I certainly wasn't expecting a call from anyone. Every time my phone rang though, no matter what, a brief yet intense surge of "what if" exploded deep in my brain.

I was up to my old tricks having recently sent Trudi a "thinking of you" card on which I wrote a carefully crafted message with obvious ulterior motives.

Dear Trudi,

Fall is such a beautiful time of year. I remember the trees surrounding your house and how, at the time of my visit, they were coming back to life with the gentle pastel colors of spring. I know they must be breathtaking with the bolder, blazing colors of fall. I am teaching literature at one of my favorite places on earth and am doing fine. I hope all is well with you and your family. I have not spoken to Connor in many years but, as you know, he is never far from my thoughts. I pray that he is well and happy. Please call sometime when you can 757-522-3236 as I would love to catch up.

Sincerely,

Lucy

I was praying that my words would inspire a conversation with her beloved son about me which would then prompt him to call. It appears that card resulted in my exact intention.

The letters G-E-O-R-G-I-A scrolled across the display of my phone. If life is a roller coaster then just at that moment I reached the crest and at the sound of his voice on the other end of the line, I was on a free-fall that no coaster in existence can compare to. The time had come to get what was mine. I had put in so many patient hours and it was finally paying off.

"Hello?" I said trying to keep some measure of cool.

"May I speak to Lucy?"

"This is she."

We were both laughing like tweens before he could say, "Hey, it's Connor, remember me?"

"I...um...of course I remember you."

"Well, it's time we figure this thing out," he said. I felt like he was finally on board, like me. Yes, it had taken a long time but the last pieces of the puzzle were falling right into place. I was certain that Connor and Lucy were back.

We had to see each other and quickly. It was November and I wanted to seal the deal before the New Year. See, I had no doubts. Twenty years didn't matter because it was Connor. Life was giving me a fairytale. The magic hidden behind the message was about to make sense of my love story. It was about to make sense of my life. I could just imagine my little night dancers performing a very happy dance for me. I had let him go and although it took twenty years, he was back. But there was more to his story than mine.

I had some growing up to do and I aged significantly during our meeting in Atlanta. He bought my plane ticket and two nights at a gorgeous, romantic five star hotel in the city. Connor had found his talent working in a high-stress environment beyond the suburbs; something about sustainable energy. He told me that he was "blessed, very fortunate," but I wouldn't have cared if he was struggling from paycheck to paycheck. The man of my dreams was back, my first and only love.

My life seemed to be opening up like a flower in the sun and I felt a happiness I had not experienced since before our short love affair ended twenty years ago. I was ready now to accept his proposal unlike when I received it before at eighteen. How fortunate to get a second chance. So I packed my carry-on bag, my letter just in case I needed it, and every bit of naïve optimism I could conjure in my fractured little heart and flew south to reunite with Connor Hawthorn.

I arrived at the hotel and checked in about three hours before he did. I showered and put on the short black dress I bought for this occasion with the black, four inch heels Mary and Tory had bought me to show their support for my life finally getting underway. He called to let me know he was near so I waited by the door in the stylish lobby. Just as the sun was setting, he pulled his silver Audi up to the curb and quickly made an exchange with the valet.

Oh my God. There he was. After endless nights of praying that our paths would cross, there he was walking toward me, Connor Hawthorn, after all these years...sunglasses, cap on backwards, thick sweater and jeans. My knees were like water and my heart was pounding out of my chest. No one except him could ever affect me this way. He was my own personal electric charge. We embraced on the street in front of the hotel without saying a word for several priceless moments. It felt like he was finally mine but I still had so much to learn.

The elevator ride to the third floor should have been my first clue because he stood with his hands in his pockets, looking down at the floor. It was a moment of awkward silence. But I refused to be wrong this time. He freshened up in the bathroom for a minute, and then said, "Let's go see what this city has in store for us tonight." He wanted to walk around, get some dinner and maybe some coffee afterward.

"Okay, let's go," I said. Whatever he wanted he was getting if I could provide it.

The lightest snowflakes were gently falling just outside the big window front of Starbucks where we sat on opposite sides of a tiny round two-seater leaning in to hear each other under the soft jazz. It had been twenty years and there he was. I was not disappointed. Time had changed the young boyish looking soldier I knew into a grown man. His hands were still rough, and his body was still tight and muscular. His blonde hair was longer than a military cut, still short but long enough to show the curl on top. He ordered his coffee black and added five packets of sugar at the table. I can remember that detail but I can't remember a word that was spoken. I'm pretty sure it had something to do with how time has flown and how much we seem the same. What did I say? What did he say? It's better remembered in silence anyway: the dim lights in our cozy corner, the white Christmas lights strung in trees that lined the busy street, the people passing while their winter coats and scarves flapped in the biting wind. The wintery world beyond the glass seemed to be moving in slow motion as I sat there spellbound by the only man I have ever loved.

I had flown to Atlanta to spend two days with Connor, just the two of us after all those years and if he had asked, I would have said, "yes." Just like that. The years didn't matter to me. It was right in my world. His spirit seemed to still be intact even after suffering three marriages, each ending in divorce. I knew why he had divorced those women so it didn't matter to me; in fact, I was the reason. He was looking for me, not them. That was my fantasy and I wasn't letting go.

We walked back to the hotel huddled close together with his arm around me. When we entered the room, I noticed a bottle of Merlot and two wine glasses waiting for us on the table. "I can't believe how much you still look the same," he said while pouring two glasses half-full. I wondered about that comment because I knew twenty years had certainly taken its toll.

"You too," I said from the bathroom where I was nervously slipping into my version of something more comfortable.

He soon joined me on the foot of the bed and we sipped our wine, smiling at each other, feeling awkward with that strange tension of who would make the first move. Not much time passed before he took my glass and placed it with his back on the table. He sat down and caressed the side of my face. I closed my eyes savoring this moment I had been dreaming about for so many years. Then he kissed me. It wasn't the same innocent, apologetic kiss we first shared in the dim light on Judd Street but it still wrapped me in chills. He laid me back. I inhaled his scent and felt every nuance of his body. Conner Hawthorne had come back to me...and I was ready.

Things were going just as I had imagined they would. I mean, there was an understandable lack of emotion on his part (it had been twenty years after all). There were no tears or "God, I love you, Lucy" whispered into my ear. And the way he just disappeared into the bathroom afterward; so what. It gave me a chance to finish my wine, pour another glass and finish that one too. Hindsight is such a bitch.

We found there wasn't much to say since we had already told each other our own vague, selective stories of the past twenty years during our recent phone conversations. So I just lay in his arms while the TV flashed on the wall like a strobe. I was feeling of his skin, conscious of my fingertips moving over his chest which had actually sprung a few hairs over the years, confident that this was the first of many nights together; possibly the rest of our lives.

I did not sleep, but he finally did. I remembered being in D.C. many years ago and waking-up to McDonalds on the morning before our first time together. I longed for the innocence and purity of the love we shared back then.

Promptly at 7am he got out of bed without acknowledging my existence.

"Good morning," I said, sitting up under the white sheet pulling my knees in close. "Good morning, Miss Bells."

"Um, we need to have a serious talk today about some important things." I actually had the nerve to get all giddy and excited like he was about to plan our wedding or talk over possible names for our kids. At some point don't you think I should have received a sign from God; just a little omnipotent kick of reality? The truth is I could have received a text from Jesus himself saying, "Run, now, back 2 NC." It would not have changed my mind. I was determined to be right about Connor and me.

"Get ready, okay? I'm going out to get us some coffee and bagels. I'll be back."

I quickly showered and got dressed in my carefully chosen outfit. I was going for relaxed and nonchalant yet sexy and cool in my gray cashmere V-neck sweater, my broken-in Levi button flies, and black high-heeled boots. I looked as good as I possibly could; much better than I looked in D.C. when our love was young. I was more mature now, more stylish, and I wore expensive facial moisturizer, designer perfume, and a nice watch...

whatever. It really didn't matter. I was about to have a serious talk about some important things with Connor.

We drank coffee from paper cups and ate bagels knee-to-knee, fully dressed, sitting in chairs. "So, did you enjoy yourself last night?" he asked.

"Yeah (that was a little weird), did you?"

No reply. Then he began, "I remember when I first saw you sitting Indian style in your corner chair on Judd Street. You were so pretty in your little flowery shirt, the way it was untied and open, showing off your sexy collarbones. You stared at me for, like, ten seconds and I believed you were my soulmate."

"Yeah, I remember that," I added, as chill bumps covered my body with that sweet recollection. "I believed you were mine too."

"Of all the mistakes I've made, and I've made plenty, you were not one of them. I loved you, you know." I inhaled slowly, deeply... ready.

He cupped my right hand between his hands like he had done after our first "real talk" on the front porch of the Judd Street house twenty years ago and began, "I just have to come out and say this the way it is and there is no easy way to tell you, no gentle way to put it, Lucy, I'm in a relationship and she's pregnant." The words came so calmly and quietly out of his beautiful mouth, so gently and apologetically, yet their effect on me, on my entire internal being was something like a meteor burning through Earth's atmosphere, speeding toward the ground and exploding into a deep, dark cloud of debris and emptiness.

My heart sank to the pit of my stomach. I had no idea how to react; burst out crying, run to the bathroom, congratulate him, bend over in agony. So I just sat there expressionless, ears ringing from my internal explosion, while Connor finally let me go.

"I think I know what you wanted from this trip and I'm pretty sure it's the same thing I wanted, but I can't walk away from what I have now. I wanted to see you, to be with you one more time because I just needed to know for sure for myself. You have always been a burning question in the back of my mind and I thought that if I...if we...well, I know the answer now and I cannot continue to let us hang on to this. I have moved on and I want a life without secretly wondering about you. And I want to be a father. I'm forty-one; time's running out on me. I wanted that with you many years ago but we were too young. I'm different now and I'm not your perfect soldier anymore. I'm sorry if I've hurt you again. I know this was selfish. I'm selfish, but you already know that about me."

(No, I don't. I know that you like a Sweet-n-Low in your milk, that you like your PB&J with more jelly than peanut butter, that you like to eat Capt'n Crunch with chocolate milk. I know that you're perfect in my eyes.)

"Say something. Don't you want to, like, slap my face or something? I understand if you do. Trust me, I won't stop you."

Here I go again. I have no words, only the memory of Pan's broken heart in black ink losing its birds over a raging black sea. I knew that was meant for me. My omen from Pan the very first moment I laid eyes on Connor. So this is reality and I have nothing. I have no slap for his face, no congratulations, no desperate begging for it to be a lie, just nothing. All I can see in my masochistic mind is another woman on his arm and pregnant with his baby.

"Hey, I know you're disappointed," he said as he reached up to wipe the tear that was rolling down my expensively mois-

243

turized cheek. I looked at the table because I couldn't look at him. I took note of the coffee I would not finish drinking and the bagel I would not finish eating. I looked at my left-hand fidgeting with the stylish hotel pen; the hand that would never wear his wedding band after all. I wondered if he was having a boy or a girl. What name would they choose? I imagined him at the T-Ball stand coaching like it was the major leagues, only it wasn't me on the sidelines this time.

"The truth is, Lucy, I still love...I still care about you and I always will. But what we had, what we shared before it all went wrong, is the one thing that will always be perfect for me. I can't risk fucking that up now. Sorry, my damned mouth. God, sorry."

Even at this devastating moment he managed to bring a smile to my face. I sat up on the edge of my seat and hugged him around his neck. He relaxed and hugged me back. It felt like a yearning for things to be different. It felt like disappointment on both our ends.

I rubbed the long stubble on the back of his head. "I'll call the front desk to get a cab. I'm going home." I closed my eyes and kissed his lips one last time, feeling his burning cheeks with my cold hands, forehead to forehead. His lips weren't mine but they had been once upon a time before my fairytale ended twenty years ago.

He was right; he wasn't my perfect soldier anymore. The truth had unmasked him. One devastating glance revealed his aged skin, rough and wrinkled from sun and stress. His once emerald eyes, now mellow gray. His spirit had been tamed from years of unhappy endings. I wanted to bring my Connor back around, but I had to let him go. Once again, it felt like this time was finally the last time. Connor was a grown man, not running or searching anymore. He had gone out into the world and welcomed new love. He had risked hurting again and again, while I never did. I believed in us. I bet my life on us.

One last embrace and then I boarded the cab painfully aware of having lost that bet. Against my better judgment, and incapable of resisting, I turned around in my seat, and watched him standing there on the sidewalk in front of the hotel. I watched while he disappeared in a golden, glaring ray from the morning sun. He let me go, free-falling into the world without him, my unrequited, only love.

I arrived in Atlanta fragile like a sheet of shattered glass barely holding together. I left in a million tiny pieces, disoriented, fumbling, and alone; finally, alone. Yes, I *have* always been wrong except for one thing: my heart undoubtedly and irrevocably belongs to Connor Hawthorn and always will.

At the end of another failed trip to get Connor back, my silver linings were waiting at the end of the concourse. Mary and Tory were prepared to receive me with a bottle of wine and my favorite "Boys Don't Cry" cupcakes. We all cried and wished things had been different. They told me I had to move on. I agreed with them; all of us doubting behind our half-smiles, knowing behind our sad eyes that I never would.

CHAPTER 38

I would have said "yes," but you didn't ask
Twenty years spent holding the past
Like a parent who can't let go
Like denying the one thing you know
I would have said "yes," but you held it in
All this time waiting for life to begin
Like waking up to not know your own face
Like training your whole life to lose the race
A simple question, "Will you marry me?"
I would have said, "Yes, Connor, finally."
No need to wait anymore
You finally closed the door
The sun rises yet what shall I do?
All I know is waiting for you

I'm sitting here alone in my little white house in my little college town wondering what is wrong with me. What keeps my heart from changing, from healing? Everything changes and heals eventually. Even a forest cut down and burned will, overtime, teem with rebirth welcoming life again. And the mirror's reflection is a most enthusiastic agent for change. My once *naturally* black hair is trying hard to hush the gleaming silver strands screaming that I'm growing old. And these eyes, they can't be mine. On close inspection, I see the countless lines that surround the openings to my very soul. I blame them because they looked at him and refuse to look away. I wish they would change their view, potentially setting me free, but they only see him. They will continue to grow older while only ever seeing what has already lived and died.

It was Tennyson who published the idea that it was better to have loved and lost than never to have loved at all, but this doesn't ring true for me. I should have never loved, as even the sweetest fruit changes; becomes rotten, putrid, and toxic. This love is beyond saving and yet I hoard it in my chest like Davy Jones. It hurts when the one to whom you belong does not want you anymore. It hurts to lack the ability, the innate survival strategy, to change, live and learn, love and let go, press on, forget, heal, try again. How does this work?

And so here I am at my crossroads with my letter I could not deliver and my shattered dream understanding that my efforts to be with Connor Hawthorne will never pay off. If you love something let it go; on second thought, don't. Keep it close and pray that you will have what it takes to hold onto it. It doesn't matter if it was really yours or not as long as it is in your arms at the end of another day. Why wait to see if it comes back. Most likely, it won't. Just don't let go of what you can feel and hold. A dream leaves you wanting, empty-handed, and alone.

I have always been wrong. They were never my same fireflies coming back to me each summer. I learned somewhere along the way that the lifespan of a firefly is only about seven days. When I let them go from their little glass jar home, they would all soon die giving way to an endless cycle of renewal; a brand new company of dancers given the chance to live out their seven days of bliss in my backyard theatre. My fireflies had more to teach me about life than I was willing to learn.

Now that my story has been transferred to these pages, I am hoping for some kind of rebirth, new direction, awakening...at least some peace and quiet. I wonder, though, if these doors were opened for me all at once, would I even be willing to walk through them and leave this all behind.

The sun rose again this morning painting another master-piece. It seems that for today at least, my efforts remain futile. I am still a constant amid certainties, as fixed as the sun, as sure as the waves will crash on the beach, as constant as the ebb and flow of the tides...as faithful as my fireflies.

****

My heart belongs to someone who does not want it

Orphaned, abandoned in its prime

No entry to its only home

A homeless wanderer forced to roam

Aimless on a lingering plume

All that's left of a fire consumed

My heart, it wonders what is wrong

It beats, it loves, its conviction strong

But something keeps my heart adrift on this lonely sea

Empty and vast stretched out before me

My heart, it holds a dream so dear

Though dead and gone for many years

Refusing to wake and start anew

My heart is still waiting for you

Acknowledgements

I must first acknowledge my daughter, Sada, who has been with me through the frustration, the give-ups, and the walk-aways. She always settles me and brings me back around. Thank you, Sada, for lending an ear to my ramblings and giving me honesty, patience, and love. You are an amazing daughter and the light of my life.

Mary Hollowell, you have always been my biggest fan and best friend. Thanks for being the first one to read a dumpy, partial draft of murky prose years ago. You have always given me confidence and encouragement to keep writing. Lucy does not exist without you.

Keaton Whitehurst, you were the most intense, honest, harsh, loving, supportive reader I had. My novel is polished because of your thoroughness and time-consuming dedication to catching...well, everything. When you said you loved my book, a choir of angels burst forth in song in my head (or was that you??;)

Georges Velo Rosell, thank you so much for helping me with my French! Your intelligence, humor, class, and worldiness have endeared you to my heart forever. You gave me insight from the outside regarding my main characters... something I needed. You will say, "I'm undeserving, ma chère," but nothing could be further from the truth.

Mama, it meant everything to me when you read my book and wrote a note expressing how much you loved it and how proud of me you are. That will always be one of my most treasured items. Without your approval, this would all just seem incomplete.

Wayne and Bonnie, thank you for supporting me in all my endeavors. You are the best siblings and I'm grateful for you.

Thanks to all my friends who have read a draft of this book. Your reveiws helped build my confidence and I am proud to have you on my team.

ABOUT THE AUTHOR

Laura Hollowell

Laura resides in Norfolk, Virginia with her daughter and teaches US History in middle school. A native of North Carolina, she proudly received her BA from the University of North Carolina at Chapel Hill. Return of the Fireflies is her debut novel.